Falling

from

Fire

Falling

from

Fire

Teena Booth

WENDY
LAMB
BOOKS

Published by
Wendy Lamb Books
an imprint of
Random House Children's Books
a division of Random House, Inc.
1540 Broadway
New York, New York 10036
Copyright © 2002 by Teena Booth

Wendy Lamb Books is a trademark of Random House, Inc.

Visit us on the Web! www.randomhouse.com/teens
Educators and librarians, for a variety of teaching tools,
visit us at www.randomhouse.com/teachers

Library of Congress Cataloging-in-Publication Data

Booth, Teena.

    Falling from fire / Teena Booth.

    p. cm.

    Summary: Fourteen-year-old Teri is trying to find out where she fits
in, both at home and at school, and when her house burns down in a
fire, she thinks she may get a fresh start.

    ISBN 0-385-72978-2—ISBN 0-385-90047-3 (lib. bdg.)

    [1. Fires—Fiction. 2. Identity—Fiction. 3. Family life—Fiction.
4. Mothers—Fiction. 5. Schools—Fiction.] I. Title.

PZ7+

[Fic]—dc21

                           2001050694

The text of this book is set in 11.5-point Meridien.
Book design by Susan Livingston

Manufactured in the United States of America

June 2002

10 9 8 7 6 5 4 3 2 1

BVG

For my children

Scotty, Natalie and Evyn

So that they may know

how amazing they are

chapter one

I still dream about the fire. I wake and my throat feels swollen and scratched, my lungs hurt and my hair reeks of smoke. I am halfway out of bed and flailing against the blankets before I realize it's only a dream. Then I look around my new room at Gramma's and—I can't help it—I laugh.

Gramma says things always happen for a reason. (Except for Grampa dying when he slipped on the icy sidewalk and hit his head on the mailbox; she says that happened for no reason at all.) I spend a lot of time wondering why the fire happened. In my mind, I keep turning back to it and going through the whole thing again. I watch the flames shoot out of the windows toward the black sky. I feel the heat rolling from the house in waves. I feel my shock like a hard ache in my chest. I also feel the urge to elbow someone and say, Can you *believe* this?

I want to understand it, how it happened, how it changed everything the way it did. Sometimes I stop and wonder, What would I be doing right now if our house was still there and I was still in it? I always see myself sitting there on the peach-covered couch, staring at the TV, or making up lists of things I didn't like about myself.

My mother acts like the fire was the great tragedy of her life. She told me she still can't get through one day without crying about something she lost, something she wants back. When she says stuff like that, I turn my face away so she won't see how I feel. Then I change the subject.

Everyone says we're lucky no one died in the fire. I think it had more to do with the smoke alarm than with luck. And if it hadn't been for me, the smoke alarm might not have been working that night.

Back in sixth grade the Timberville fire chief came to our school and passed out orange Junior Fireman booklets. He said that if we did all the assignments in the book and passed a test, we could be junior members of the fire department and get real fire hats. I knew my brother, Andrew, would go nuts over the hat, so I did all the assignments in the book. I still remember that you can't put too many plugs in an outlet and that you're supposed to crawl on your hands and knees beneath the smoke. And if you catch on fire you're supposed to stop, drop and roll.

The Junior Fireman booklet also said you're supposed to hold a family meeting to talk about what to do in case of a fire. That was back when my mother was married to Bill Rickman (or as my sister, Samantha, called him, Beer Belly Bill). Bill worked the swing shift at the mill, so we had to wait to hold the meeting on his night off, which happened to be the Monday night the Raiders were playing the Broncos.

Samantha was fourteen and going through what my mother called her pissed-off stage. I remember she had just started wearing her black baseball cap, pulled low over her eyes, all day, every day, even in the house. She shoved every scrap of her blond hair under that cap so you couldn't even tell she was a girl.

That night Samantha sat on the couch with her knees to her chest, repeating, "This is so lame." Andrew was only two and he was galloping around saying, "I'm a horsey," and making snorting noises.

"Look, Andrew," I said to get his attention. "Stop, drop and roll. Stop, drop and roll." Andrew laughed and flopped onto the stained green carpet to roll after me.

Samantha sighed extra loud. "This is why I missed going to the movies with Maxie?"

"Oh, hush," said Mom. She was sitting next to Bill, on the arm of his recliner, and her bracelets jangled as she smoothed the blond wave of her hair back into its curve against her cheek. "We all have things to do, Teresa, so let's get the show on the road."

I pushed myself up and walked on my knees to the coffee table to spread out the diagram I'd drawn of the house. "Okay. In case of a fire we all have to know the nearest exit and an alternate exit."

Samantha rolled her eyes. "You just go out the window, genius."

"Sounds like a plan," said Bill. He raised his can of Budweiser as if to toast such brilliance, then picked up the remote control and switched on the game.

My mother snatched the remote away and clicked off the TV. "Can't you leave it off for five minutes?"

"Look," I said, pointing to the diagram. "The front door is the nearest exit to the bedrooms. The back door is the alternate exit. And we're supposed to pick a spot to meet outside so we know we all made it out."

Bill scratched his beard, then reached for the remote. Mom cried, "God!" and wrenched the remote away. "I'm going to throw this thing away, I swear it!"

"Hey!" Bill yelled back. "I get one lousy night off a week. I can spend it any way I want."

"Stop, drop and roll!" Andrew shouted, and rolled into the dining room table so hard that he toppled a bowl of cereal left over from that morning. The bowl landed on him and he rose up, shrieking, his dark hair covered with soggy Cheerios and spoiled milk.

Mom ran to help him, Bill turned on the TV again and that was the end of the meeting. Later, Mom signed the assignment page in my Junior Fireman book anyway, so Andrew got his fire hat.

For the next two weeks I sniffed around the house

like a fire station dog, looking for hazards. I even got up the nerve to ask Bill to check the battery in the smoke detector, but Mom kicked him out before he got around to it.

I didn't run across the fire hat again until a year later, when Mom was about to marry Lenny Brungard (who Samantha dubbed Skinny Lenny) and I was looking for my white sandals for the wedding. Andrew wore the hat to the wedding rehearsal at the park, and when we got home, I went around the house looking for worn cords running under the carpets. I also asked Lenny to change the battery in the smoke detector. That was when he still cared if us kids liked him or not, so he grabbed a chair and a screwdriver and took the cover off the smoke detector while I stood beside him, ripping the plastic off the new battery.

Now I wonder what would have happened if I hadn't got Lenny to change that battery. Maybe if it hadn't been for me, we all would have died a horrible death the night our house burned down. But then again, if it hadn't been for me, the fire probably wouldn't have started in the first place.

chapter

two

Before the fire, there were three last names on our mailbox. My mom was still Jeanette Brungard, even though she had divorced Lenny six months after they had gotten married. (He said having three kids around made it impossible for him to meditate; Mom said fine, go meditate someplace else.) Andrew's last name is Rickman because Bill is his father. And me and Samantha's last name is Dinsmore even though our father moved back to his hometown in Texas when I was three.

I don't really remember my father, although I've talked to him on the phone a few times. He has a soft half-voice, as if some of his vocal cords are missing. Mom says it was his voice, all wrapped up in a Southern accent, that made her notice him in the first place.

My mother and father met when they were both seniors at Timberville High, the same high school I go to now. They sat next to each other in American history, and he would let her cheat on tests by showing her his paper. Mom recorded their whole courtship in her diary, and she made a rule that as soon as we turned eighteen she'd let us read it. But, like everything else, it's ashes now.

Luckily, Samantha turned eighteen in January, two months before the fire, and on her birthday she brought Mom's diary into our room to read some of the juicy parts out loud.

"I've never known a boy like him," Samantha read. *"Tonight he did the most marvelous thing. He got on his knees and asked to kiss the hem of my skirt."*

"Ugh!" Samantha tossed the diary aside and threw herself backward on her bed. "I can't stand it, I really can't."

My eyes moved to the diary, a regular spiral-bound notebook, at the foot of her bed. I was desperate to know what happened next. I leaned across the gap between our beds and grabbed for the diary.

"Ahem," said my mother from the open doorway. She had one hand on her hip and the other pointed toward the notebook, pink-polished fingers waggling.

To Samantha she said, "I see I was wrong in thinking you were mature enough to read about me and your father."

"Oh, come *on*." Samantha sat up. "Who wants to read about their parents making out? It's gross."

Mom looked down at her diary and smoothed the pages. She didn't often get angry but she was easily hurt if we failed to appreciate her or something she'd given us. And Samantha always went out of her way to fail to appreciate Mom.

"I want to read it," I said. "I'm mature enough."

Mom didn't say anything. That meant it was probably too late to make her feel better. Any minute now, she'd give us both the same betrayed look, lumping us together as "you girls," then go shut herself in her room.

But Mom just arched a brow at Samantha and said, "I hope you're not wearing that hat to dinner."

Samantha's eyes were hidden in the shadow of her baseball cap, but the corner of her mouth twitched in a smile. "It's *my* birthday dinner, shouldn't I be able to wear what I want?"

It wasn't what she said but the *way* she said it that made me want to rip the cap off her head and make her eat it. I wouldn't, of course. Samantha might have been petite like Mom, but she was strong. And wicked mean. It never paid to pick a fight with her.

"I know what I'm wearing," I rushed to say. "My Irish sweater." The sweater had been one of my Christmas gifts from Mom. She always smiled when I wore it, and she smiled now as she turned away from Samantha and said, "Why don't I French-braid your hair for you?"

I gasped, "Really?" She hadn't braided my hair in months and months.

Mom motioned for me to follow her into her bedroom. I made a face at my sister, then danced along after Mom on a bubble of glee. Normally Mom's room was off limits to us. Only when she was "between men," like she was then, did she allow us to go inside with her.

I loved my mother's room, with its big picture window like a frame around the evergreens in our backyard, which were blanketed that day in snow. I loved the huge bed covered with lacy pillows. I loved the walk-in closet full of belts and hats and silky scarves and high-heeled shoes in a pile of colors. I especially loved the vanity with the little pink stool and the mirror with the lines of lightbulbs running up each side. The bulbs gave off a soft, misty light that painted everything with a sheen of perfection.

It was a magic mirror, and as Mom dragged a crackling, staticky brush through my hair, I sneaked looks at my reflection. I liked the little jolt of surprise I felt to see that my usual self was not looking back. My real self, the one I normally saw in the bathroom mirror, was plain and colorless except for red dots of pimples scattered across my chin. But there, in my mother's mirror, my face actually seemed acceptable. And my hair didn't appear to be its usual dishwater blond but looked deep gold and shiny, almost like Mom's.

No, scratch that, I thought as my eyes moved up to watch my mother separate my hair into strands. My hair wasn't like hers. My mother's hair was a lemony white-blond and fell to her shoulders in graceful waves. Gramma called Mom's hair her crowning glory. Gramma also considered Mom's hair good advertising for Dorinda's Beauty Salon, the shop she owned and worked in with Mom.

Mom's hair also helped her reputation as the most beautiful woman in town. True, Timberville was pretty small (population 1,809), stuck way up in the Trinity Alps in Northern California. But still, there were lots of pretty women here, and everyone said Mom was the prettiest. They even made it official each summer by voting her Best-Lookin' Gal in Town during Old Miners' Festival Week. One year the newspaper actually described her as "Timberville's very own Marilyn Monroe," and went on and on about the way her platinum hair caught the sun and the eye.

People often stared at her whenever we went anywhere, which was sometimes kind of fun, like hanging out with a movie star. Then there were the times my sister was there, too, and people would remark how interesting it was that Samantha looked so much like Mom, and I—well, I must take after my father. Samantha had got all Mom's looks, Samantha, who hid under a baseball cap and had a loud, obnoxious laugh and didn't even *care* about what she looked like.

Mom tilted my head down so I couldn't see her in the mirror anymore. I closed my eyes to savor the feel of her deft fingers working my hair into the braid, but she was already almost finished. She was, after all, a graduate of Redding Beauty College and head stylist at Gramma's salon. She could lace up a French braid in about two minutes flat.

Mom tied off the braid, then stepped away. I turned

round on the stool to look up at her. "Could you put some makeup on me? Just a little?"

She gave me a look that said I must be kidding. Gramma would be coming to dinner with us, and we both knew Gramma's rule: Properly brought-up girls don't wear makeup before they turn sixteen. I was still fourteen.

I put my hands together in a praying position. "Please, please, pretty please?"

"Well. All right, just a little." She turned the chair to kneel in front of me, then began dabbing makeup on my cheeks with feathery touches of her fingertips. I inhaled the smell of powder and perfume, then let my breath out in a happy sigh.

"So you want to read my diary," Mom said finally.

I nodded. "Can I?"

"Head still. Close your eyes. No, you can't read it, not yet. But if there's something in particular you want to know..."

"Everything," I breathed. "I want to know everything."

I felt her smile, and although she didn't tell me everything, she did tell me a lot. Like how she wouldn't give my father the time of day for months because she was part of the Rebel crowd and my father was a Bible Thumper.

"So then, you were a Rowdy and he was a Holy Roller?" I asked.

"Well, whatever you kids call them now." She took my chin in her hand to turn my face first one way, then the other. "You'd think by now they'd come up with a couple more cliques just for variety's sake."

"You'd think," I agreed. But I also knew that in a school with only 150 students, fewer than 40 per grade, there really weren't enough of us to make up a bunch of different groups. Although Samantha did tell me that in her freshman year some kids tried to form themselves into an arty group. But since most of them smoked pot, they ended up hanging out with Rowdies.

"Anyway," Mom continued, "your father wasn't part of my crowd, so I tried to ignore him. But it's not easy to ignore someone with a voice like that. And besides, he was so good-looking, in that yummy blond Leif Garrett kind of way, if you know what I mean."

I had no idea who Leif Garrett was, but I nodded as visions of Doug Stewart, a boy in my California history class, passed like a parade float through my mind.

"No matter how much I pretended not to like him," Mom said, "he kept following me around and writing me little poems. He said he could feel my heart whispering to him whenever I looked at him."

Then one day, Mom went on, my father stood outside her bedroom window and began singing to her in his rough-soft voice and said he wouldn't stop until she granted him a kiss.

"That's exactly how he put it, too," Mom said. "I had

to *grant* him a kiss. So I went outside and told him I wouldn't kiss him until he *granted* me a friendship ring. He said he would, but in the meantime..."

Mom sighed and sat back on her heels with a dreamy look. "He kneeled right there in the wet grass and asked if he could have the honor of kissing the hem of my skirt. And he did, he kissed my skirt like it was something sacred. And that was it for me, baby doll. I fell in *love*."

"Oh my God." I pressed my hands over my heart. "Just like a movie."

Mom's soft look faded. "Yeah, just like a movie. Boy meets girl, boy talks girl into eloping to Reno, boy gets girl pregnant at eighteen, then again before the first one's out of diapers. Then boy can't find a good job and tries to drag girl off to Texas, and when girl doesn't want to go, boy gets even by refusing to send child support. Some great movie, huh?"

I didn't say anything. I'd already heard the ending a hundred times.

Mom gave my face one last stroke of a powdered brush. "There. All finished. What do you think?"

I stared into the mirror at a girl with smooth, Natural Peach–tinted skin, eyes that looked deep green in smudged Sienna Brown outline, cheekbones that showed up in a slant of Rosy Plum blush. I could not take my eyes from the mirror.

I barely noticed when Andrew burst in, crying over a

bump on his head. I barely noticed when Samantha came in and argued with Mom about where we should go to dinner. I just kept gazing into the mirror and thinking that if I could look like that, then maybe other things were possible, too.

See, what I didn't tell Mom was that even though there were still only two main cliques at Timberville High School—the Rowdies and the Holy Rollers—there was also a third group, a nongroup, made up of all those who didn't fit in anywhere else. They were called the Nobodies, and that's what I was: a Nobody. I wasn't sure how it had happened, because I'd hung out with the same group of girls all through middle school. But once we walked through the doors of Timberville High, half our group went the Rowdy direction, half went Holy Roller, while I went nowhere. Within a few weeks I'd found myself walking the halls alone, invisible to my former friends.

So far I'd been too depressed about the situation to do anything about it. But maybe, if I could go to school as the girl I saw in my mother's magic mirror, people would simply start seeing me again all on their own. Sitting there on the pink stool in my mother's bedroom, I tried to picture how it would be: walking down the hall at school, people waving and saying hello; Doug Stewart asking me to sit with him at lunch.

I went on to imagine school dances and dates and all kinds of other things. But I never once, not even for a second, imagined the part about the fire.

14

chapter three

The morning after Samantha's birthday, I found my mother in the kitchen in her filmy purple bathrobe, bent over in front of the open refrigerator.

I planted myself at her elbow. "Mom, I've been thinking, and I really think I'm old enough to wear makeup to school. Lots of freshmen wear makeup, lots and lots."

She straightened, milk jug in hand, and shut the refrigerator door. "Not going to happen."

"Just a little? Please?" I danced around to stand in front of her. "I'll clean my room every single day. I'll do the dishes every single day. I'll take Andrew to the park every single—"

"Teri," Mom interrupted. "You heard the fuss your grandmother made at dinner last night. The last thing I need is her lecturing me morning, noon and night on—"

"I won't let her see it on me, I swear."

Mom stepped around me and went to pour some milk into Andrew's cereal bowl. "Give it a rest, will you?"

"Mom!" I wailed. "You don't understand!"

"Oh, really," she said lightly. "I was fourteen once, too, you know."

Hearing that only made me feel worse. I'd seen pictures of her at fourteen and she'd been gorgeous even then. I crossed my arms over my chest. "Yeah, and *you* had a boyfriend when you were fourteen."

Then Samantha stepped into the doorway from the living room. "*Waa, waa*, poor Teri. No one likes me, I'm so ugly."

I glared at her. "Shut. *Up.*"

"It's a little early in the morning for cruelty, don't you think?" Mom said as she moved back to the refrigerator to put the milk away.

Samantha leaned a shoulder against the doorjamb. "I don't see why you don't let her wear a little mascara or something. It's not like you care what she does."

Mom frowned at her over the open refrigerator door. "How can you say such a thing? Of course I care."

"Not if she wears makeup you don't. You only care about getting grief from Gramma."

Mom's face started to close up in her hurt look.

I stomped toward Samantha. "Will you please *butt out*?"

"I'm only trying to help," she said innocently. I knew better. She was only trying to get at Mom, not help me. She didn't understand my life any better than Mom did. She belonged to the Rowdies, she was pretty and she'd had her first boyfriend by the time she was twelve.

I looked back at Mom. "I'm sorry I brought it up. I don't want to wear makeup. Just forget the whole thing."

As I pushed past Samantha to get out of the kitchen, I heard Andrew saying, "*I* want to wear makeup. Can *I* wear makeup, Mommy?"

Back in my bedroom, I zipped on my heavy jacket without looking in the mirror, then tiptoed back through the hall toward the living room. I was hoping to slip out the front door unnoticed, but I found Mom waiting for me.

She moved toward me with a watery-eyed smile. "You know I care about how you feel, don't you, baby?"

My stomach hurt when she sounded like that. I quickly nodded and said, "I know," without even thinking about it.

Mom looked relieved as she reached up to brush my bangs away from my forehead. "I really do understand what you're going through. Everyone wants to be liked. And I know it's hard when you're a late bloomer, but believe me, honey, someday soon the boys are going to sit up and take notice of you."

I couldn't get out the front door fast enough. If there is one thing worse than being an ugly duckling in a house of swans, it's having the swans pretend there's no difference.

When I pried open the back door of the ancient school building, a wall of noise hit me so hard it made me wince. Because there were only eight class-rooms in the school, the entire student body crammed into one short hall between classes, and voices echoed double loud off the high, cobweb-covered ceiling.

After I skirted a clump of seniors standing in the middle of the hall as if they owned it, I spotted Wesley Wilton waiting for me by my locker. I winced again.

Wesley's coat was half on, half off, and he was trying to cram a notebook into a suitcase-sized backpack that was already jammed too full. "You were supposed to meet me in the library this morning." He grunted as he gave his notebook another shove. "We were supposed to start outlining our report."

I sighed. Wesley and I were assigned to the same bi-ology project and we had immediately clashed over how to go about it. I wanted to hurry and get it over with. He wanted to take it slowly and methodically, as if our comparing different cell structures was on the same level as finding the cure for cancer. When I'd suggested that we compromise, he'd delivered a speech about how one should never compromise one's education.

I nudged Wesley aside so I could open my rust-streaked locker. "I never said I would meet you."

He hoisted his backpack up to his shoulder, notebook still poking out. "Well, we'll just have to meet at lunch, then." He stepped around me to head down the hall.

"I didn't say I would!" I called after him, but he just

kept walking as if he hadn't heard me. I slammed my locker. He was the most maddening person I'd ever met.

Wesley's nickname was Prez because he let it be known that he planned to be president of the United States someday. A lot of kids made fun of him over it, but that didn't seem to bother him. For instance, one day around Thanksgiving some of the Rowdies surrounded Wesley at lunch and asked him if he'd make drugs legal when he became president. They snickered like it was a big joke, but Wesley merely closed the book he'd been reading and said, "Yes. We could tax them and cut down the budget deficit. Then we could clear out the drug backlog in the judicial system, and I believe it would go a long way to solving the gang problem, too." That shut them up.

That was back when I used to admire him, back before I knew him very well. Now I knew that although Wesley might lead the country someday, it wouldn't be as president. It would be as dictator.

The first bell rang, making my heart lurch. A strange pressure began building in my chest. California history was my first-period class, my first class with Doug Stewart, and as I approached my classroom, the pressure sank down into my stomach. I took a deep breath, then stepped through the doorway.

My eyes jumped to Doug's seat, across the aisle from mine. He was already there, slouched at his desk, flipping a pencil in the air. A shaft of sunlight slanted down from a high window directly onto his head, making him look golden all the way to the tips of his eyelashes.

Doug had moved to Timberville over the summer, and although he hadn't known a soul before September, he'd been instantly accepted into the Holy Rollers. And he was so nice, so polite, that even the teachers adored him. He definitely outclassed everyone else, as if his real parents lived in Beverly Hills and he'd been sent to live with the poor relations in Timberville.

I walked to my seat through a tangle of hope and fear that he might look up and smile or say hi. Of course he didn't. He never did. And of course I didn't say hi to him, either. I just sat, staring ahead and listening as he told Jake Bloom he hoped there wasn't a quiz that day because he hadn't studied, and was it true that Stacey Sorenson used to go out with Terrence Gatling?

Only when class started, and Mr. Reginald with his jumpy, hairy eyebrows began lecturing about the beginning of the Mexican War, did I finally ease back into my seat and let my head turn slightly toward Doug. From the corner of my eye I could see his blue-sweatered arm resting on the edge of his desk as he turned his pencil between his fingers in a slow circle.

As I watched the spinning pencil, hypnotized by the movement, I remembered what Mom had said that morning about me being a late bloomer. Maybe she'd been right. Maybe any day now, I would wake up and find myself a swan. Maybe then Doug would sit up and take notice when I walked into the room. Maybe then he'd ask me out, fall in love with me. I couldn't help grinning as I tried to imagine him kneeling at my feet, the hem of my skirt in his hand. . . .

The pencil in Doug's fingers had stopped turning. I looked up to find Mr. Reginald looking expectantly at me.

"I'll repeat the question, Teri," he said. "Why do you think Captain Fremont camped with his army outside Monterey after being ordered by the Californio government to leave the colony?"

I had no idea what he was talking about, and as several people turned their heads toward me, prickles of heat crawled up into my face. "I don't know," I finally mumbled.

"See me after class," Mr. Reginald said before asking if anyone, anyone at all, had an opinion about Captain Fremont's actions. Half a dozen hands shot up and Doug's pencil started turning between his fingers again.

I slumped down in my seat. It was probably a good thing that Mr. Reginald had stopped my daydream before it had gone too far. Before Doug had talked me into eloping to Reno and having babies. Before he had abandoned me to go back to Beverly Hills and I found myself stuck in Mom's life.

It was definitely time to cut back on daydreaming. I sat up straight to focus on Mr. Reginald and the Mexican War.

chapter
four

After Mr. Reginald informed me that I was barely passing his class, I went to biology and found out our lab projects would account for half our grade. I decided I'd better meet Wesley to work on our report after all.

I found him sitting at one of the tables crammed into the open space in the middle of the library. He didn't look up from the paper he was writing on as I dropped my backpack on the table and pulled out my notebook. I slid into a chair, dug around for a pen and then flipped open my notebook.

"Okay," I said. "What do we do first?"

Wesley held up a finger, which clearly meant *Don't interrupt, genius at work.* He scribbled a few more words, then slid the paper to me. "Finished. This is your copy. Read it tonight and we'll start working on the report tomorrow."

I looked down in surprise. "The outline? You did the whole thing?"

"Obviously."

"Then why'd you make me meet you here if you'd already finished it?"

He looked at me as if I was a dim-witted child. "I hadn't finished it when I asked you to meet me."

I huffed, sending the sheet of paper sailing off the side of the table.

"Great," I said, then had to lean over sideways and twist myself into a pretzel to reach it. When I'd worked my way back up to the table, I found Wesley pulling a book from my backpack.

"Hey!" I yelled, and snatched the paperback away.

"I'm just curious to see what kind of books you read," he said.

I folded my arms over the book. I was too embarrassed to let him see that it was a cheerleader romance. Mom had given me a whole box of them for Christmas and I couldn't stop reading them.

"Have you ever read *Treasure Island*?" Wesley asked. "Or how about *Huckleberry Finn*?"

"I doubt it."

Wesley sighed and started lecturing me on the importance of reading good literature while young. It was a typical Wesley Wilton lecture, full of long words and a superior tone, which was kind of funny coming from a boy who couldn't remember to comb his hair. Or maybe he did comb it, but it was black and wiry and so short that little clumps of it stuck straight up. Which was too bad, because Wesley was actually a decent-looking guy, with nice gold-brown eyes that always looked kind of red and warm and sleepy from reading late into the night.

Wesley must have noticed that I wasn't listening, because he quit talking and grabbed for the book. We struggled over it until he squeezed my wrist so hard that I yelped with pain and let go.

"That hurt!" I said hotly, rubbing my wrist.

Wesley ignored me while he turned my book in his hands. He made a *tsk-tsk* sound, then tossed the book back at me. "If you're going to read that kind of stuff, you may as well watch television."

I stuffed the book back into my backpack. "Isn't my choice of reading material protected by the Constitution?"

"Does your mother know you read that junk?"

"My mother *gave* it to me, so you can just shut up."

Just then Randy Mellon, one of Wesley's friends, stopped at the table. "Okay, kids," Randy said. "Enough fighting. Time to kiss and make up."

I gave an exaggerated shudder. "I'd rather eat worms."

But Wesley only looked at me and said, "If you want, I could lend you my copy of *Treasure Island*. It's a very good book."

I blinked at him. Was our argument over already?

Wesley stood and said, "I'll bring it tomorrow." Then

he walked off with Randy while I sat there, rubbing my wrist.

Later that evening, just as I was digging through my backpack for the outline Wesley had written, Mom knocked on my bedroom door and asked if I wanted to watch a movie with her and Andrew.

"I finally found *Snow White* under the couch," she said breathlessly. "We haven't watched it in ages."

I jumped up to follow her into the living room. It was always fun to watch Disney fairy tales with Mom. She knew all the songs by heart and would pull us off the couch to dance around the living room with her.

That night we danced together to "Someday My Prince Will Come." Mom had to stand on tiptoe to twirl me beneath her arm. Then I twirled her until we fell to the couch, laughing and dizzy. Then it was Andrew's turn, and he marched around the coffee table behind Mom to "Heigh-Ho." He kept marching even after the song was over, and he didn't stop until the wicked queen turned herself into an old woman. He scrambled onto Mom's lap to watch, his brown eyes growing wide.

"No! Don't eat it!" he shouted when the hag held out the poisoned apple. And when Snow White took a bite, Andrew's face grew bright red beneath his freckles. "She shouldn't have done that."

Mom laughed and stroked his head. "Aw, baby, it's okay. True love is worth a little bit of poison."

When Prince Charming kissed Snow White awake at the end, Mom sighed happily. "Now, that's a prince. But I think *my* Prince Charming would have blond hair."

"Yeah," I said, thinking of Doug. "Mine, too."

I forgot all about reading Wesley's outline until the next morning when I turned away from my locker and found Wesley standing behind me. I was racking my brain for a good excuse when he thrust a paperback at me. He let go and I had to grab it to keep it from falling to the floor. It was *Treasure Island*.

"I didn't say I wanted to read it!" I called as he walked away. Of course, he acted like he didn't hear me.

I added the book to the others in my arms as I walked to California history. As usual, I felt a pressure in my chest when I saw Doug, and as usual, he didn't even glance my way. I took my seat, and as we waited for Mr. Reginald to fill up the blackboard with notes for us to copy, I picked up Wesley's book to look at the pictures of pirates on the cover.

Something brushed my shoulder. I raised my head to see Doug leaning out of his seat across the aisle to peer over my shoulder.

"Hey, *Treasure Island*," he said. "That's a great book."

The elevator inside me dropped down, then shot back up. I heard myself say, "Huh?"

"Yeah, I read it like in eighth grade or something. Have you read it yet?"

I shook my head.

Doug leaned his cheek on his fist. "I still remember Long John Silver. He was a riot."

Then Mr. Reginald turned from the blackboard and barked, "Page ninety-three, please!"

I tried, but I couldn't find page ninety-three. I just kept turning pages and replaying the entire one-sided conversation in my mind. Doug Stewart had spoken to me.

Of course, he wasn't much like Prince Charming, who probably wouldn't have cussed under his breath when quiz papers were handed back and he saw the D he'd earned.

chapter
five

For the rest of the day, nothing bothered me. Not Wesley scolding me in biology for neglecting to follow his orders, and not Samantha telling me to get away from her when I tried to sit with her at lunch.

"How many times do I have to tell you?" she snarled. "Don't talk to me at school."

"What a small person you are," I said before I walked away with a sad shake of my head.

She was small, but I was big. I was so big that other people could now actually see me. Doug Stewart had seen me. Doug Stewart had talked to me. And most wonderful of all was the possibility that he might talk to me again.

The next morning as I walked to school, the cold biting at my cheeks, I imagined getting to class and Doug asking me about the book and what my favorite part was. By the time I started across the school parking lot, we had moved on to discussing the various movie versions of *Treasure Island*. Then, just as I was confessing that the only version I knew had been done by the Muppets, I rounded the back end of a pickup and nearly slammed into two people wedged into the narrow space between parking slots.

As I stumbled back a step, I realized it was Doug leaning against the truck. And standing between Doug's wide-planted legs was Stacey Sorenson.

Stacey and Doug looked perfectly posed there against the snow, two beautiful blond people in color-coordinated knitted caps and ski jackets, wearing identical just-kissed looks. I told myself to turn around but I stayed stuck to the spot, ankle-deep in slush and gaping at them through the fog created by the blasts of my breath.

"Hey, Teri," Doug said finally. "How's it goin'?"

"Um . . ." I shrugged.

Stacey gave me a cool up-and-down look before stepping away from Doug. "It's too cold. Let's go in."

"See ya," Doug said, then turned to walk off with his arm around her waist.

I automatically started walking along behind them, which is how I heard Stacey whisper into his ear, "Are you friends with *her*?"

That stopped me. That made me bend over to catch my breath. I crouched that way for a long moment, watching as a clump of snow on my boot melted and dripped off the side of my foot.

The first bell rang, sounding thin and hollow against

the thick damp of the air. Class would start in five minutes. I stood outside for another four, shivering violently. Then, just as I turned to go in, an old black Camaro in need of a muffler rumbled into the lot and stopped just outside the doors. Samantha jumped out of the passenger side with a lit cigarette in her hand. She took one last drag, then reached back into the car to hand it to the black-haired man inside.

It wasn't until the car swung back around that I recognized the driver. Brian Webber had graduated a few years earlier and now worked in the hardware store. He was notorious in Timberville for having been busted for possession of cocaine at the age of twelve.

As the car drove away, Samantha looked over at me. First she gave me a fake smile. Then she shoved her middle finger up in the air and whirled it.

I wanted to yell "I hate you!" so everyone could hear. But Samantha was already heading into the building and class was starting in less than a minute. I hugged my coat tighter around me and hurried in after her.

That afternoon it was my turn to pick up Andrew from After Care at the elementary school. Heavy gray clouds crowded out the sky, and it was starting to get dark as we walked up the hill from Main Street. As we passed by Gramma's beauty shop, Mom ran out to walk us the rest of the way home. She came up between us with a cheerful "Brrr! It's freezing!" Then she slipped her arm through mine and squeezed it to her side as if I was her best girlfriend.

Right away I knew she'd met someone. She always acted like me and Samantha were her best friends when she met someone she liked. This meant we would soon be entering what Samantha called the Fresh Boyfriend Phase (as opposed to the Stale Boyfriend Phase). The upside to a new boyfriend was that Mom would usually be in a good mood. The downside was she'd be gone every other night, which meant me and Samantha would have to take turns baby-sitting Andrew.

"So tell me," I said to my mother as soon as we got into the living room. I dropped into an overstuffed easy chair and draped my legs over the arm. "What's his name?"

She gave me a sly smile. "You're not going to believe this, but it's Nolan Redmond."

I had to admit, I was impressed. Nolan Redmond was the most famous former resident of Timberville. He'd been a football star at Timberville High around the time Mom went there; then he'd become a football star at a big university in the Midwest. A few years later he started writing sports murder mysteries and so far had gotten three of them published. Whenever a new one came out, the Timberville Book Stop would hold a signing and the whole town would turn out to line up the length of Main Street. The chief of police would have to stand in the street to keep traffic moving.

Mom was standing with her hands on her hips, waiting for a reaction.

I widened my eyes. "*The* Nolan Redmond?"

Samantha came in from the kitchen with a bag of tortilla chips. "What about Nolan Redmond?"

Mom sank onto the couch with a happy sigh and told us how Mrs. Redmond, Nolan's mother, had rushed into the beauty shop without an appointment because her son was coming for a visit.

"You know how she is," Mom said. "The Queen of Sheba herself, demanding that we all drop everything."

Then Nolan, on his way to his mother's house, had seen her car in the parking lot and stopped in to surprise her. According to Mom, Nolan had a ton of thick blond hair and when she had teased him about needing a haircut, he'd helped his mother out of Mom's chair and slid into it himself. By the time she whipped the plastic curtain off his neck, he'd asked her out to dinner for that very night.

Mom let her head fall back against the couch. "He said he used to be wildly infatuated with me in high school. He said the only reason he never asked me out was because I was a year older and he was afraid I'd laugh at him."

"Or he was afraid Daddy would beat him up," Samantha said as she stuffed a chip into her mouth.

Mom giggled, then reached for the bag of chips. "Now here it is, almost twenty years later, and he's asked me out. It's like fate, don't you think? It's like everything in both our lives was working toward this one inevitable moment."

"You know," Samantha said, "that's the exact same thing you said when you met Skinny Lenny. You said it was fate that made you both reach for the same loaf of banana bread at that bake sale in front of the post office."

Oh, how I wanted to kick Samantha. Listening to Mom tell her tale had been like listening to a bedtime story, and I'd begun to feel warm and sleepy and far away from my unpleasant morning. Now Samantha had ruined it, now Mom would feel hurt and—

But Mom just groaned and put her hands over her face. "You're right. I did say that, didn't I?"

Samantha snorted with a laugh. "Do you remember the first time Lenny came to dinner and stayed in the bathroom for nearly an hour?"

As the day dimmed at the windows, I sat warm and drowsy while the two of them passed the bag of chips back and forth, making fun of Lenny between bites. Andrew came in a few times and flew a toy airplane over their heads before disappearing into his room again.

"Honestly, Mom," said Samantha. "I don't see why you had to marry him. He didn't even have a job."

"He did so," said Mom. "He had that gig at Chavonne's every Friday night, remember?"

"Strumming on a guitar in a coffeehouse once a week is not a job," Samantha said.

"Maybe not. But when a man sits at your feet with his guitar and sings love songs to you, well, you kind of lose your head."

"So what did Bill do to get you to marry *him*?" Samantha asked. "Sit at your feet and burp in your face?"

Mom slapped playfully at Samantha's leg. "No, silly. Don't you remember how much fun Bill used to be before Andrew was born? We all went camping together, remember? And the day he took us out on the lake on his brother's boat?"

"I remember that," I said. "I remember I got seasick."

"Yeah, and I remember the look on Bill's face when you barfed on his foot," Samantha added, which got us all laughing so hard that Mom almost choked on a chip.

Then the front door opened and Gramma came in, carrying a paper bag. We all got quiet, as if we'd been caught doing something wrong. I don't know why. Gramma didn't act like anything was wrong. Her face seemed perfectly blank, as usual. Gramma had the ultimate poker face; I could never tell what she was thinking.

It was hard to believe that someone like Gramma could be related to someone like Mom. Even though they had the same green eyes, they looked nothing alike. Mom liked to wear cherry red and electric blue;

Gramma wore beige and black. Mom liked to sweep her hair up into intricate knots; Gramma kept her gray-brown hair cut in a straight line across the back of her neck. Gramma was one of the few women business owners in town and she liked to carry herself with the dignity of her position. Mom liked to lick her thumb and stick it to her hip with a sizzle sound, telling people she was "too hot to handle."

Still, Mom and Gramma had a strange ESP thing between them. Each could always tell what the other was thinking, and the only way I knew when Gramma wasn't happy was that Mom got quiet and stiffened up. Like she was doing now.

Gramma set the paper sack on the coffee table. "You forgot your shampoo."

"Thank you, Mother," Mom said. "It was nice of you to drop it by."

"It was no trouble." Gramma's eyes took in Mom and Samantha sprawled on the couch, covered with chip crumbs. Her face still seemed blank to me, but Mom sat up straight and snapped, "Why don't you just say what's on your mind?"

Gramma carefully folded her hands in front of her. "All right, I will. Helen Redmond is a friend, and I know a few things about Nolan that you may not. He has a disastrous history with women, Jeanette."

Mom's chin lifted and she gave a brittle smile. "Well, my history with men is not so wonderful, either."

"Which seems to me a recipe for certain heartache between the two of you."

Mom struggled to her feet. "Why, Mother?" she asked in a wounded voice. "Why do you do this? Why do you tear me down every time I try to be happy?"

"Nonsense. I'm merely concerned for you. I'm concerned about the way you continue to fling your heart open to inappropriate men—"

"Inappropriate!" Mom yelled. "We're talking about Nolan Redmond!"

I flinched at Mom's voice and pressed myself deeper into my chair. But Gramma held her ground even as Mom advanced on her.

"There's not a single person in this town who would call Nolan inappropriate. I don't understand why you . . ." Mom's wobbly voice trailed off, then grew loud again. "Is this because Daddy died and left you alone? So now you want me to be alone, too? Is that it? You want me to be a bitter, lonely old woman like you?"

Gramma sucked in her breath at that. Even I could tell she'd been hurt. And Mom could tell, too, because she began backing away, tears filling her eyes. My own eyes felt hot with tears as I watched her turn and run toward the hall. A moment later the bookshelf rattled from the slam of her bedroom door.

I felt as if a fist was clenched inside my stomach, but there was Samantha, calmly reaching for another chip.

"You know, Gramma," she said. "If I was you, I'd slap Mom's face for talking to you like that."

I flew at Samantha, yelling, "If you don't shut up, I'm going to slap *you*."

"You're the one who'd better shut up," Samantha said. Then she stood and slugged me on the shoulder. I crumpled to the carpet, holding my shoulder while I breathed through my clenched teeth.

"That's enough!" Gramma clapped her hands together like an angry teacher trying to get the attention of her class.

We both looked up. Her face had regained its usual composure and her voice fell back into calm as she said, "If a person is going to stick her nose where it doesn't belong, a person ought not be surprised to find her efforts unappreciated."

Gramma zipped open the purse hanging on her shoulder and began digging through it. "You might think that after all these years I'd know better than to try to talk your mother out of disaster. How are you supposed to protect your children from themselves? You can't."

She finally pulled her keys out of her purse and zipped it shut. "You have to sit there and try to understand that when a girl is only thirteen and her father dies on the sidewalk in front of the house, it creates a hole that can't be filled up, no matter how . . ."

Gramma stopped, looking at me and Samantha as if she'd just remembered we were there. "Look who I'm talking to. Girls with no father at all. The irony is not lost on me."

She shook her head and said, "Tell your mother I'll see her tomorrow." Then she turned and walked out.

Samantha and I were left alone in the sudden quiet. I wanted to yell at her for hitting me, but I had no energy left. I could only sit there and watch as she got up to take the half-empty bag of chips into the kitchen. I could only sit there as the room grew darker and darker and my mother still didn't come out of her room.

chapter
six

By the following week, Mom and Nolan were deep into a serious relationship. Mom made a point of telling Gramma all the nice and gentlemanly things Nolan did; Gramma made a point of acting pleased. But Gramma declined Mom's invitation to go out to dinner with us to officially meet Nolan.

Samantha tried to get out of it, too. I heard her arguing with Mom in the hall from where I kneeled in front of our messy closet, digging for my left boot.

"Forget it!" Samantha yelled. "I'm not going on any more tryouts for any more of your stupid boyfriends."

"Samantha," Mom said. "It's just dinner."

"Do you know that in some families the boyfriend actually has to try out for the kids?"

"Try out?" Mom repeated. "Why do you keep saying that? I have no idea what you're talking about."

"Big surprise!" Samantha stormed into our room and slammed the door behind her.

A moment later, Mom threw the door open and stepped inside. Her hair was up in a swirl of ringlets and she was wearing a tight red dress that matched her lipstick perfectly.

Mom's eyes shone with tears. "Don't do this to me, Samantha. This is too important. If you ruin this for me, I'll never be able to forgive you."

Mom stepped out and closed the door. Samantha stood in the middle of the room, shifting from one foot to the other, arms crossed like taut ropes over her chest.

"You should come," I said as I stuffed my foot into my boot. "It might be fun."

"Ha!" Samantha flung her arms out to the sides. "It'll be a nightmare of embarrassment. She's thirty-six years old and she still thinks she's freakin' Cinderella."

She stood there shaking her head for a long minute. Then she ripped the baseball cap from her head. "Now I have to take a shower. Holy Christ!"

Later I couldn't figure out why Samantha had bothered to take a shower, because by the time Nolan rang the doorbell, she was back in the same baggy jeans and baseball cap. Mom looked at her with lips smashed together, but she didn't say anything as we all trooped out to Nolan's BMW for the quarter-mile drive to Timberville's only steak house.

The restaurant was the closest thing to fancy that Timberville had. There were linen tablecloths and napkins, and on the table there was a lantern-style candle, which Andrew kept trying to touch until Mom finally blew out the flame. Nolan ordered a plate full of appetizers with onions and mushrooms and stuff that none of us kids liked. Mom kept giving me a look and tilting her head toward the plate until I finally picked up a mushroom and stuck it in my mouth.

"Is that the best stuffed mushroom you ever tasted, or what?" Nolan said in his loud, football-player voice. Everything about him was loud and big. He seemed almost too large to fit in the booth. In his bulky sweater, his arms seemed inflated like cartoon arms. Samantha took a crayon from the cup the hostess had given Andrew, and on the corner of his place mat she wrote, *The Incredible Hulk lives.*

By the time the dinner plates arrived, Samantha still hadn't said a word. She didn't even crack a smile at Nolan's story about how he'd convinced an editor at a big publishing house to read his first novel.

"I found out the editor's favorite football team, got the quarterback of that team to autograph a ball, and two weeks later"—he snapped his fingers—"I've got an offer for a book contract."

Nolan laughed big, Mom laughed bigger, and even Andrew did a convincing job of cracking up. Samantha just rolled her eyes.

Finally Nolan excused himself to go to the men's room, and as soon as he was out of sight, Mom jumped up and pointed to the door.

"Samantha, I want you to leave. Go home. Now."

Samantha's jaw dropped. "But I'm not done eating."

"I don't care." Mom grabbed her by the wrist and yanked. "You haven't said one civil word to Nolan. Why should he buy you dinner? Now, go!"

Mom kept pulling at Samantha's arm until she half fell out of the booth. "Okay!" Samantha snapped as she got to her feet. "Fine! I told you I didn't want to come in the first place!"

Half the people in the dining room turned to watch her stalk toward the door. Mom gave a flustered smile and loudly said, "Teenagers. What can you do?"

Someone chuckled; then everyone turned back to their own tables. Mom sat down, smoothing her hair. Andrew turned his mouth down and slowly dissolved into tears.

"You yelled at Samantha!" he cried. "You shouldn't yell! She's my sister."

Mom quickly leaned to stroke his head, whispering, "Be quiet, honey, please be quiet and we'll order you some ice cream for dessert, okay?"

By the time Nolan got back to the table, Andrew was done whining and Mom was leaning back in her seat as if nothing had happened.

"Aren't we missing someone?" Nolan asked as he sat.

Mom pursed her lips in a pout as if she expected him to be angry with her. "Honestly, the way she was acting. I had to send her home."

"You know who she reminds me of?" he said.

Mom slapped at his arm. "You'd better not say what I think you're going to say."

He leaned close to her with a big white-toothed grin. "Yep, you. She's all attitude, just like you were in high school."

Mom giggled and blushed. I put my fork down, my appetite gone.

"You should have seen your mom at school." Nolan winked at me. "Dressed in those little cheerleader outfits, turning her nose up at everyone."

"Nolan Redmond," said Mom. "I was never a cheerleader and you know it."

His hand moved under the table toward her. "I must be remembering how you looked in my imagination."

Mom squealed and pushed his hand away. "Nolan! The kids!"

I was already scooting out of the booth, dragging my coat with me. "You know, Mom, I'm done eating, and if it's okay with you, I think I'll walk home, too."

Mom and Nolan turned their heads in unison and looked at me as if they'd never heard such a good idea.

"All right." Mom slapped at Nolan's reaching hand again. "Why don't you take Andrew with you?"

"Ice cream!" Andrew wailed. "You said!"

Mom elbowed Nolan. He pulled out his wallet and handed me a twenty-dollar bill.

I took the money and picked up Andrew's coat. "Come on, Andrew. We'll stop at Maggie Moo's on the way home."

Nolan put his arm around Mom's shoulders and they both smiled and waved big goodbyes as if we were heading out on a ship. Andrew waved back as I zipped up his coat for him, and he was still waving as I pulled him out of the restaurant into the dark.

Just outside the doors we found Samantha standing by the pay phone, smoking a cigarette. In the dim light from the restaurant sign I could see that her face was red and her eyes were puffy. She'd been crying. I pretended not to notice.

"So," she said. "Cinderella and the Hulk banished you, too?"

I shrugged. "Sorta kinda."

She took a drag from her cigarette. "Brian's picking me up. If you want a ride."

"Thanks, but I have to get Andrew some ice cream."

"Whatever."

It was too cold to stand around talking, so I said, "See you at home," then started across the parking lot, Andrew's hand in mine.

Maggie Moo's Ice Cream Parlor and Sweet Shoppe was a short way down Main Street. When we opened the door, a bell jingled and the sugary smells of vanilla and fudge rolled out. The inside was warm from the hot air blasting out of a big heater mounted in a high corner.

Andrew and I stood in line behind a family I didn't recognize. The little boy rode on his father's shoulders to better see inside the glass ice cream cases, while the mother and daughter stood with heads together, reading the flavors from the menu. When it was our turn, I grabbed Andrew under the arms and heaved him up so he could see through the glass. He chose rainbow sherbet, one scoop. I ordered a hot fudge sundae with two scoops of butter pecan.

We sat at one of the tiny round tables next to the family. They talked and laughed and compared the way the girl patiently stirred her ice cream into a liquid before she ate it with the way the boy gobbled his so fast it made his head hurt. Then the mom leaned over to wipe chocolate from the boy's face with her napkin.

I looked at Andrew licking his cone, green-and-orange sherbet melting on his hand and running over the sleeve of his coat. I looked down at my own melting sundae. Then I got up to throw it into the trash.

chapter
seven

On Valentine's Day Doug and Stacey were voted the King and Queen of Hearts and were crowned at the Freshman/Sophomore Sweethearts Dance. I wasn't at the dance, so I didn't see it. But I heard about it from Wesley at school the following Monday.

Wesley always went to school dances because his mother, Irene Wilton, was president of the PTA and the first to volunteer as chaperone. A big joke at school was that since Wesley never showed up with a girl, his date at the dances was his mother. He'd even go out on the dance floor with her. (Although one girl did tell me that the mother-son dancing team was so good that they sometimes got applause.)

Anyway, Wesley filled me in on all the gory details of the coronation of the King and Queen of Hearts while we put our lab equipment away in biology. He told me about how Stacey's tiara had slipped from her head and rolled under the stage, and how Doug had crawled in after it. He told me about how they'd danced together to the love theme from *Titanic*.

"Oh, and I suppose you were dancing with Mommy at the time," I said.

I'd forgotten Wesley was insult-proof. "No, not Mom..." He frowned, trying to remember. "I believe I was dancing with Corinne at the time."

"Corinne Bailey?" I asked in surprise. Corinne was one of Stacey's best friends.

He nodded. "She's in my youth group."

My face grew inexplicably hot. "Oh," I said, then turned away.

I had forgotten Wesley was part of a churchgoing family. Which, of course, meant he belonged to a youth group. All Holy Rollers belonged to youth groups that met once a week to study the Bible and talk about God. They also had barbecues in the summer and went on ski trips in the winter.

More than anything, I wanted to be in a youth group and have instant friends and learn about God. But it was genetically impossible. My sister was a Rowdy and my mother had been the Rebel version of the same thing. No one in my family ever mentioned God, let alone set foot in a church, and I didn't know how to approach one alone. All I knew about religion had come from the lady with the pink wig and false eyelashes who prayed into the camera every day on the Christian cable station.

I was glad when the bell rang. I hurried into the hall and ducked into the girls' bathroom. I dropped my books to the floor, then turned on the faucet in the ancient, chipped sink. As soon as cold water touched my face, I felt better. Then a toilet flushed, one of the stall doors creaked open and Stacey stepped up to the sink beside mine.

I froze, face dripping water, while Stacey leaned forward to inspect her reflection in the mirror. A wrap-around cranberry-colored shirt ended far enough above her hip-huggers to show off a strip of her belly, but not so far that she'd get sent home.

Her eyes flicked to mine; then she straightened up and turned to me. "Hey, you're Jeanette Brungard's daughter, aren't you?"

The question was so unexpected that all I could do was stare.

"She did my hair for the dance and I saw your picture on her little counter thing," Stacey said.

"Oh."

"I never knew she was your mom. I mean, you don't look like her."

I yanked a paper towel from the holder. "So I've heard."

Stacey turned back to the mirror to gaze at herself. "I don't look like my mom, either. Thank God," she added as she leaned over her sink to wash her hands. "She weighs, like, two hundred fifty pounds. She sits on the couch all day, never goes anywhere. It's disgusting." She shuddered as she reached for a paper towel. "Your mom is beautiful. You're lucky."

I squeezed the paper towel in my hand into a ball. "I guess."

"You know, it's funny." Stacey looked back in the mirror, tilting her head to one side, then the other. "I look more like your mom than you do."

I gave her a weak smile. "Maybe we were switched at birth."

Her head snapped around. "When's your birthday?"

"Stacey," I said. "I wasn't serious."

"Mine's June fourth. When's yours?"

"March fifteenth." I was surprised at the spurt of relief I felt. Had I actually been afraid it was true?

Stacey looked anything but relieved. She turned back to her reflection, muttering, "Stupid, stupid."

"No," I said. "You do look like my mom. You have the same hair color and everything."

"You mean this?" Stacey grabbed a handful of her hair. "This isn't my hair color. This is Ash Blond Number 8B. My hair is really light, *blech*-y brown. Just like *my* mother's."

The bathroom door opened and three other girls filed in. Stacey immediately leaned into the mirror and checked her teeth with a bored look.

I tossed my paper towel into the trash and picked up my books. As I left, I lifted my hand to wave to Stacey, but she didn't glance my way.

That afternoon, I walked straight to Gramma's beauty salon. Like half the businesses in Timberville, the salon had once been a house. It looked a lot like our house on the outside, a big white-painted rectangle with low windows and a small cement porch. But inside, the living room was now the waiting room, and the sinks and haircutting stations were divided up, two to a former bedroom. It smelled like hair chemicals and coffee and nail polish and hair spray. It smelled like Mom and Gramma mixed together.

Mom wasn't there, but I found Gramma in one of the haircutting rooms, sweeping white hair across the white linoleum. I dropped into one of the chairs under the dome of a hair dryer and blurted out, "I want to dye my hair."

Gramma stopped sweeping and stood the broom up in one hand to regard me.

I pressed on. "I want it Ash Blond. Like Mom's."

"Absolutely not," she said.

"C'mon, Gramma. Please?" I'd expected to have to beg. "I'll look so much better."

"You look fine."

"No, I don't."

She crossed her hands atop the broom handle. "Does it mean that much to you?"

I nodded solemnly.

Gramma shook her head, then went back to sweeping with hard, fast strokes. "You're your mother's daughter, all right. She was always complaining about her hair when she was your age. It was too thin, she said. She talked me into giving her a permanent, then hid in her room for three days because she thought it made her ugly. I won't make that mistake again."

Gramma stopped sweeping and pointed the end of her broom at me. "I'll tell you what I told her. If you start thinking who you are is what you look like, then what are you going to do when you grow old?"

I rolled my eyes toward the ceiling. What did getting old have to do with anything? "Can I get my hair dyed or not?"

"Do you have forty dollars?" Gramma asked. "Because that's how much it will cost you."

"Gramma!" I cried. She knew I didn't have any money. But by the set of her face I knew she wasn't going to give in.

I got up and stomped toward the door. "Fine! I'll just stay invisible for the rest of my life!"

I ran across the beauty shop parking lot to my house, then banged through the front door. I was halfway across the living room when Mom's voice stopped me.

"Something wrong, Teri?" she asked from where she sat on the floor beside Andrew. They were coloring in one of Andrew's old *Sesame Street* coloring books.

Must be Guilt Day, I thought. That's what Samantha called the one or two days a week during Fresh Boyfriend Phase when Mom made a point of staying home to spend time with us. On those days she turned into a TV mom and would clean house and bake cookies and ask, "How was your day, sweetie?" I usually looked forward to Guilt Day, and I usually joined in on coloring book sessions, too. But not today.

"It's Gramma!" I said in a huff. "Because of her, I can't wear makeup. Because of her, I can't dye my hair. I don't see why she gets to run my life!" Then I ran to my room before Mom could say anything.

I lay in bed for the next hour, switching back and forth between being mad at Gramma and making myself do my English homework, which was to finish reading Shakespeare's *Julius Caesar*. "Beware the Ides of March" Caesar was warned before everyone he knew stabbed him in the back. My eyes moved down to the footnote. The Ides of March was March 15, my birthday. Great.

Mom knocked on my halfway-open door and stepped inside. Her arms were locked behind her back, and her lips pressed together to hide a smile. "I have a surprise for you."

I closed my book and sat up.

She brought her arms round in front of her and held out something covered in bright orange and yellow flowers. I didn't know what it was, although it looked familiar.

"My old makeup bag," she reminded me.

"Oh!" I jumped up, took the bag into my hands and opened the zipper. Inside I saw a bottle of Cover Girl foundation, a pink tube of mascara, a brown eyeliner pencil and several eye shadow compacts. They were all half-used, but still.

I threw my arms around Mom. "Thank you, thank you, thank you, thank you."

She laughed and said, "You have to promise me you won't let Gramma see any of that stuff on you."

"I promise." I hugged the bag to my chest. "Cross my heart and hope to die."

An hour later we were sitting at the kitchen table, spooning chicken stir-fry onto our dinner plates, when Samantha came in with the makeup bag. She tossed it onto the table.

"This was in our room," she said to Mom. "Andrew must have stolen it from your bathroom."

"Did not," Andrew said.

I grabbed the bag and tucked it up next to my plate. "It's mine. And who gave you permission to take anything off my dresser?"

"Well, *excuse* me." Samantha sat at her place and picked up a butter knife to point at me. "Better not piss me off, or I might tell Gramma about your little makeup stash."

"Not if you know what's good for you, you won't," said Mom. Then she looked at me and we smiled across the table at each other, two women who knew how to keep a secret.

The next morning I spent half an hour locked in the bathroom, putting on my new makeup. I wanted to look exactly like I'd looked the day Mom had put makeup on me, but no matter how carefully I applied the mascara, one eye always seemed to show up darker than the other. I kept adding until my eyes looked about even, then stepped back to blink at my reflection. I wished I could have asked Mom her opinion, but it was her day to open the beauty shop and she was already gone.

As I walked to school, my eyes felt sticky and strange. I wasn't used to seeing my own eyelashes, and I kept reaching up to pluck clumps of black stuff off the tips. Still, I liked feeling different, and as I headed into the school building, I felt my chin lift and my stride lengthen.

I had just tossed my hair over my shoulder when I saw Doug and Stacey heading my direction, their fingers twined in each other's belt loops. My chin drooped back toward my chest and my eyes hit the ground.

I stepped back to let Doug and Stacey pass and somehow ended up stepping on Wesley Wilton's clean white Reeboks.

"Ow!" he said.

"Well, what do you expect?" I snapped. "Sneaking up on me like that."

"I wasn't—" He bent to peer more closely at me. "Hey. What's wrong with your face?"

I put a hand to my cheek and glanced toward Doug and Stacey, who had stopped only two feet away. "Nothing's wrong with my face."

"Well, you've got big black circles under your eyes," he said. "You look like a raccoon."

I tried to punch him, but I missed. I was sure Doug and Stacey had heard the whole thing. I turned and hurried down the hall and into the rest room.

Wesley was right; with flaked and smudged mascara ringing my eyes, I did look like a raccoon. I turned on the water and pushed up my coat sleeves to wash the makeup away. I didn't even care that I was late to California history.

I decided the only way to punish Wesley was to ignore him for the rest of my life. I began that day in biology, staring blankly at the wall when he asked me what my one-act play for English was going to be about. Naturally, he didn't notice that I was ignoring him. He just plowed on about possible plots for his own play.

"What do you think of an imaginary account of Franklin Roosevelt's third presidential campaign in which the campaign manager is an undercover Nazi?" he asked.

I made an exaggerated turn toward the clock.

He picked up my pen to examine the writing on its side. "Or do you think I should do something a little more abstract?"

Clearly I would have to say something this once.

I snatched my pen away. "I think you should just leave me alone."

His head came up in surprise. Then his face reddened as he turned away.

I slammed my pen down on my desk. How dare he look hurt! He was the one who had humiliated me! And he hadn't even apologized! How dare he act like *I* was the bad guy!

And yet the look on his face stayed with me throughout the morning, and by the time I left geometry I was in full regret mode for snapping at him. After all, Wesley at least *saw* me in a school where everyone else, including my own sister, looked right through me. If it hadn't been for him, I probably would have gone through the entire day looking like a raccoon without anyone saying a word.

As I turned from my locker, I spotted Wesley in the mass movement of students toward the cafeteria. When he drew near, I fell in step beside him.

I handed him the copy of *Treasure Island* he'd lent me. "It was too long."

He added the book to the stack in his arms. "That's because you have the attention span of a three-year-old."

And just like that, everything was back to normal.

Well, not exactly normal. That day at lunch, as I came out of the lunch line with my loaded tray, Wesley waved me over to where he always sat with Randy Mellon.

"What?" I said, thinking he meant to ask me about our biology homework or something.

He scooted over, making room for me. I stared down at the empty space in slow surprise.

"Are you going to stand there all day?" he demanded.

I sat.

Randy grinned at me, showing a half-chewed bite of food. He pointed his hot dog at Wesley. "You have to excuse him. He was raised by wolves and hasn't learned how to behave in public yet."

"So *that's* the reason," I said. "I thought it was a mental handicap or something."

Wesley's elbow banged my arm as he took the paper cover from his straw. "Oh, sorry," he said with exaggerated innocence. "Did I hit you?"

I poked his hand with my fork. "Oh, sorry, did I stab you?"

Then I picked up my hot dog and took a big bite. Normally I didn't like hot dogs much, but that day, they tasted fine.

chapter eight

One day I was eating lunch alone in my usual corner spot in the cafeteria, and the next I was eating lunch with Wesley and Randy at a table in the middle of the room. I felt so conspicuous that first day out in the middle that I half expected one of the volunteer lunch ladies to tell me to get back to my place in the corner. I knew that was ridiculous; there wasn't a soul at school besides Wesley who would notice where I sat.

But someone did notice.

"I saw you with those guys at lunch today," Samantha said in a singsong voice from the doorway of our room. I was sitting on my bed, trying to get started on my one-act play for English.

I tried to ignore her, but she jumped knees-first onto the foot of my bed.

"Come on, now," she sang. "Tell your big sister which one you like."

"Neither," I said.

She got off the bed. "Yeah, right."

Later she smirked at me across the kitchen table as

we ate the tacos she'd cooked. "Guess what, Andrew? Teri's got a boyfriend."

I sighed. "No, I don't."

"Yes, she does. And it's either Wesley Wilton or the other guy, what's-his-name."

"His name's Randy."

"Ah. Then it's Randy."

"It's *not* Randy," I said, too strongly.

Samantha smiled slowly. "Then it's Wesley."

"You're so stupid." I got up to put my plate in the sink.

Still later Samantha came up behind me as I sat on the couch watching TV. "Two boys. Not one, but two. Who'd have thought you'd grow up to be such a boy magnet?"

I flung an arm out to hit her, but she'd danced out of range. She came into the middle of the room, turned her back to me, crossed her arms and began to wiggle her hands up and down along her sides. "Oh, Wesley," she moaned. "Kiss me. Kiss me before I die!"

"Gross!" I jumped to my feet to chase her, but the doorbell rang and she bounded to the front door to throw it open. Brian Webber was standing on the cement porch. Samantha pulled on his arm and he slouched his way inside, chewing steadily on some gum. He wore an oversized green army coat, and his long sideburns curved down from beneath his knitted cap.

Samantha slid her arms around Brian's waist from

behind, then leaned her head out to look at me. "Guess what, Bri? I don't think our Teri is going to be a virgin much longer."

I made a choked sound, then slapped my hands over my burning face. I ran blindly from the room with Samantha's obnoxious laugh ringing behind me.

I might have stayed there, hiding under the covers for the rest of the night, if Samantha hadn't come in to tell me she was going out and it was my turn to put Andrew to bed.

"Go away!" I shouted. "I hate you!"

She zipped her coat. "Go buy a sense of humor, will you?"

I didn't come out of my room until I heard the front door shut, and even then I crept out slowly, still waiting to hear the rumble of Brian's car. When it didn't come, I knew they'd gone around back to the toolshed to smoke pot.

Naturally, I would pretend I had no idea what they were doing. Skinny Lenny had drilled into me that smoking marijuana was "an issue of privacy." And that if I said anything to anyone, the wrong person might hear, the cops might come crashing through the door, Mom might go to jail, I might grow up in a foster home. He made it so scary to think about that I learned not to think about it at all.

But no matter what they were doing, it was cold outside and Samantha and Brian wouldn't last long out there. I didn't want to be hanging around when they got back, so I let Andrew skip brushing his teeth and hurried him into bed.

An hour later, I was under the covers with the light off when Samantha came in. I saw her shadow groping through the dark to find her bed. She sat, staring into space for a while. Then she turned her head to me and whispered, "Are your eyes open or closed?"

"Open," I snapped.

"Ooooo," she said with a stoned chuckle. "You're still pissed."

"I don't like Randy *or* Wesley," I said. "I like—" I stopped myself before I said Doug's name.

"This may come as a shock to you," Samantha said as she pulled off her boots, "but I really don't give a rat's butt who you like."

She stood to wiggle out of her jeans. "But if you don't like anyone, well, that's too bad. You're missing out. Because I tell you what." She lay back on her pillow, still wearing her baseball cap. "Love is grand."

I snorted. "*You* love Brian."

"More than my life," she said on a sigh.

"God. You sound just like Mom."

Samantha turned her head on her pillow. "If I wasn't in such a good mood, I'd slap you silly for saying that."

I rose up on my elbow. "Nolan said the same thing, you know. He said you're just like Mom when she was your age."

"Liar."

"It's true. And you *are* just like her. I bet you anything you're going to end up a hairstylist who—"

"Screw that. I'm gonna be a graphic artist."

"No, you'll go to Redding Beauty College and work for Gramma and live in this house and Brian will just be husband number one in a long line."

Samantha was quiet for a long moment. I lay back on my pillow, pleased with myself. It felt good to get the best of her for once.

Then she laughed, a smug sound, low in her throat.

"What's so funny?"

"You. You're sooo jealous that I have a boyfriend and you don't."

"I am *not* jealous!" I said heatedly. "I've got two boyfriends, remember?"

"Oh, yeah. Randy and Wesley. Boyfriends all over the place. Which makes *you* the one like Mom."

She laughed louder this time. I turned over, face to the wall. It wasn't fair. Even high, Samantha still managed to get the best of me.

chapter nine

The first day of every month Bill Rickman stopped by to drop off Andrew's child support check, and on the first day of March he came by as usual. He also got into an argument with my mother as usual. They fought just as much since their divorce as they had when they were married, and I normally didn't pay too much attention. But even with *Animal Planet* on TV at high volume, I heard Mom scream from the kitchen, "If you don't leave me alone, I'm taking the kids and moving to Sacramento!"

After Bill blew through the living room and out the front door, I found Mom sitting at the kitchen table, gripping her forehead with one hand. Her hair was only slightly askew from the bow she'd used to gather it back. Still, it was strange to see Mom with lopsided hair.

I lurked in the doorway, waiting for her to notice me.

"What is it, Teri?" she said in a weary voice.

I had to ask. "Are we really going to move?"

"Oh, baby doll, no. I didn't really mean that." She

rubbed her head, then squinted at me. "Be a sweetie and grab me a couple of Advil, will you?"

I took a bottle of pills down from the cupboard, filled a glass with water and sat down at the table with her. She gave me a little smile of thanks before she swallowed the pills.

"Oh, I think about it sometimes," she said as she set her glass down. "Moving to a bigger town. Not to Sacramento, it's too big. But maybe down the hill to Redding . . ."

She looked up to check my reaction. It had never occurred to me that we might move somewhere else. I couldn't imagine living in a place that wasn't surrounded by mountains, or where you couldn't see baby deer tiptoeing after their mothers, or where you couldn't pick blackberries off the bushes along Main Street and eat them, still warm from the sun. Talking about it was like talking about moving to Mars.

"But the logistics of it all," Mom continued with a sigh. "It would cost us so much more to live down there. And even if I could get into a good salon, I couldn't come and go as I please, like I do here. And besides, everyone knows who I am here. *I* know who I am here, if that makes any sense."

I nodded. It made perfect sense to me. She was the Best-Lookin' Gal in Town, Timberville's very own Marilyn Monroe. Who would she be in Redding?

"But now there's Nolan. . . ." Mom gazed out the window over the sink, a small smile on her face. "He'd like us to move down there. He's hinted at it several times. But then, if I get my way, he'll be moving back up here very soon."

She looked at me and we both laughed. Mom always got her way with men, at least the ones she wasn't married to. They lined up to do her favors, from the sixteen-year-old convenience store clerk who walked to the salon every morning to bring her coffee, to Old Man Harrelson next door, who brought her fresh-cut lilacs from his garden.

"Now," Mom said as she stood to take her glass to the sink. "If only I could get Bill to stop being such a pain in the neck. We've been divorced how long now? And he still has these jealous fits."

She turned and put her hands on her hips. "Honestly, sometimes I wonder if men are worth the trouble."

Then she laughed again because, as we both knew, as far as Jeanette Brungard was concerned, men were the *only* thing worth the trouble.

The phone rang from the living room. Mom turned her head to look at the clock, then turned back to me with a lift of her brows. "That's Nolan."

The phone rang again.

"Want me to get it?" I asked.

"Nope."

Mom laughed at my look. "It's good for a man to be

frustrated once in a while. It keeps him interested." The answering machine picked up in the living room, and as Mom went to listen in on the message, she said, "If Nolan wants a snooty cheerleader, that's exactly what he's going to get."

I gazed, bewildered, at the empty doorway. Then I remembered what Mom had been like when she was dating Bill. Within a few days of meeting him, she'd started listening to country music and drinking beer and wearing cowboy boots. With Lenny, she had listened to jazz and worn Birkenstocks and eaten tofu. Now with Nolan, she was listening to '80s music and wearing short skirts and tight sweaters.

I made a face. Was that what I had to do to get a boyfriend, turn myself into someone else? I thought about Samantha. She'd had a lot of boyfriends, and she always stayed the same Samantha. But then, she'd never said she was actually in love before Brian. Would she begin to change now?

I rubbed my head. Mom was right about one thing: Guys were a lot of trouble and probably not even worth it. Look at me. I had put myself through months of agony over Doug and ended up with nothing to show for it but a ringside seat to his relationship with Stacey. Each morning in California history, I had to sit and listen to Doug telling Jake Bloom where he'd gone to eat with Stacey, what movie he'd seen with Stacey, how he'd climbed a tree outside Stacey's window so he could sneak into her room.

Maybe it was time to end my agony. Maybe I should stop thinking about Doug, stop watching for him in the halls, stop listening to his conversations. Then maybe I could stop being jealous of Stacey and get on with my life. I could be like Wesley and concern myself with important things, like the quality of my education.

I left the kitchen to shut off the TV and work on my play, which was due in two weeks. Somehow it turned out to be all about a boy and a girl, kissing and love.

Maybe boys weren't worth the trouble, but I was, after all, Jeanette Brungard's daughter. I would always believe love was worth the trouble.

I stayed up late that night working on my play, and the next day at lunch, instead of going to the cafeteria, I went to the library to write a few more lines. I was just getting started when a hand darted into my line of vision and snatched the pages from under my pen.

"Hey!" I shouted, and looked up to see Wesley holding my papers high in the air. It was almost funny, Wesley in his geeky plaid shirt and clumpy haircut, looming over me like the classroom bully. I would have laughed if it hadn't been my play he was waving up there.

I jumped to my feet and reached for my pages. "Why are you doing this?"

"I'm compelled to torture you, I don't know why."

"Well, stop it!" We were practically nose to nose as I bounced in front of him, trying to get at my play.

He stepped away and lowered his arm, allowing the pages to dangle in front of my face. "Will you let me read it if I ask nicely?"

"No!"

"Then you leave me no choice."

I lunged for the pages but he was already moving backward into the stacks where the librarian wouldn't be able to see us. I staggered after him, but the only pages I could get ahold of were the ones he held out as he finished reading them.

My skin felt scorched from the heat of my embarrassment. I had only two characters, a man named Steve and a woman named Marcy, and I put them in a hotel room on their wedding night. It went something like this:

STEVE: *I can't believe we met only three days ago and now we're married.*

MARCY: *But it seems more than three days. It seems like I've known you forever.*

STEVE: *I know, Marcy. The moment I looked at you, I felt like I was finally seeing the face that is always in my dreams.*

MARCY: *Oh, Steve. Me too.*

That was what Wesley was reading as he navigated the narrow aisles backward. I was finally able to grab the last two pages before he could finish.

He shook his head. "You read too many romances."

"Shut up!" I hugged the pages close to my chest, then headed back to my table. I was halfway there when I spotted Wesley's backpack on another table and his open notebook beside it.

I looked back at him; he looked at his table. We both broke into a run at the same time. I got there a moment before he did, but as I swooped the notebook up in triumph, he slapped his hands over it and brought it back down.

We started a tug-of-war with the notebook, arguing in exaggerated whispers.

"Fair is fair," I hissed. "You read mine, now I get to read yours."

"You wouldn't understand it," he hissed back.

"Why? What's it about? Just tell me that and I'll let go."

We stopped struggling, but neither of us let go of the notebook.

"Come on, Wes," I said. "You owe me."

"For what?"

"For calling me a raccoon in front of everybody."

Wesley opened his mouth as if to argue, then said, "Oh. So that's why you were so mad at me. I was wondering." His eyes moved over my face. "Well. You don't look like a raccoon anymore."

"Gee, thanks. So are you going to tell me what your play's about or not?"

He sighed. "All right. Just give me my notebook."

I let go and lowered myself into a chair. Wesley sat across from me and planted his elbows on top of his notebook. He leaned close like he was about to divulge a great secret. "It's about a little girl who follows an ant train into someone's backyard and gets mangled by a pit bull and dies."

I stared at him. "Wes. Don't you think that's a little depressing?"

"I knew you wouldn't understand. It's a tragedy, like *Julius Caesar*. The mangling part is just the end. The important stuff is who she meets as she's following the ants."

"Then why can't she meet a boy who will save her from the pit bull at the end?"

Wesley looked to the ceiling and muttered, "Tell me she isn't serious."

"No, really. Why can't she?"

We spent the rest of lunch arguing the question, and we were still at it as we walked together into English class. I kept trying to convince him that he should change the end of his play to something less gruesome, and he kept trying to convince me that only an element of tragedy could turn my "silly soap opera" into a true romance.

Mrs. Gober obviously overheard us, because at the end of class she called us to her desk and offered to let us collaborate on the assignment if we'd be willing to expand it to two acts.

Wesley and I looked at each other, then looked away.

"I think it would be an ideal way to explore the issues you were debating," said Mrs. Gober. "But, of course, it would be a much greater challenge, and if you feel you're not up to—"

"No, I'm up to it," said Wesley quickly. His head dipped toward me. "What about you?"

I turned to meet his eyes, but even though he was facing me, he wasn't looking at me. He was gazing somewhere over my shoulder and acting nervous or something. As if what I'd say really mattered to him. As if . . . as if he liked me.

I almost laughed out loud. Wesley Wilton liked me!

I smiled sweetly at Mrs. Gober. "Oh, I'm up to it. I'm definitely up to it."

Then I stuck my hand out to Wesley and we shook on it.

I must have lain awake for hours that night, thinking about Wesley, smiling into the dark. As far as I knew, no one had ever liked me, at least not since the fourth grade, when boys were gross. I was always the one who did the liking, who churned with half-finished feelings toward boys like Doug who I barely knew.

This was different, not *at all* like my crush on Doug, who was like some guy on a movie screen I watched from ten rows back. *This* was real. And liking Wesley (and I did like him, so much!) didn't make me feel silent and frozen and embarrassed like I felt around Doug. It made me want to laugh and yell and jump on the bed.

What would happen next? I wondered. Would he kiss me? I had to roll over and press my face into the coolness of my pillow to muffle my giggles.

Each day as we worked together on the play, I'd get the same urge to giggle whenever I thought about Wesley kissing me. And I thought about it a lot. Like on the day we were walking across the quad to the library and got into a snowball fight with the last bit of dirty snow left unmelted beneath a pine tree. Afterward, he'd stood so close to me to pick clumps of snow and pine needles from my hair that my nose grazed his chin when I turned my head.

Yet after ten days we still hadn't kissed.

At least our romantic urges were being put to good use in our play. We spent lunch periods so busy talking about it that Randy quit eating with us. We exchanged phone numbers so we could call each other with good ideas and read each other lines over the phone.

We decided Wesley would write all Steve's lines and I would write all Marcy's. It made for some strange scenes, but we believed it added to the authenticity of our characters. We switched the characters so that the boy was following the ants, since I couldn't grasp why anyone would spend a whole afternoon doing that. The part where the boy and girl met went like this:

STEVE: *Hey, watch out! You're stepping on the ants, you're killing them, snuffing out their very lives!*

MARCY: *What? Oops, I'm sorry.*

Marcy stands back and watches Steve walk slowly, head down, along the ant train.

MARCY: *What are you doing?*

STEVE: *I'm following the ants to discover their origin.*

MARCY: *I can see that. But why?*

STEVE: *Because I believe ants know more about life than humans ever could. My hope is that if I follow them long enough, I will discover their secrets.*

MARCY: *Oh my God. I had a dream about ants last night. It's like it was fate that I met you, don't you think?*

Wesley talked me into including lots of grim stuff, like Steve and Marcy meeting a clown who carried around a dead mouse. In exchange I insisted on a scene in which Steve kneeled before Marcy and asked to kiss the hem of her skirt.

We figured out how to agree on most things, but we still couldn't agree on whether the story was ultimately about love or about the search for meaning or both. We spent so much time arguing about it that the day before the assignment was due we still hadn't completed the final scene, so I invited him over to my house after school so we could finish it.

Now I wonder, if Wesley hadn't come over that day, would things still have happened the way they did?

chapter
ten

Time dragged by so slowly the afternoon
before Wesley arrived that I actually took the clock
down off the living room wall to see if it was broken. It
wasn't.

To give myself something to do, I vacuumed the living room, then the hall, then my room. I'd already
cleaned my side of the room, but Samantha's side was a
wreck. I picked up all her junk and shoved it in the
closet.

I plopped down on my bed, then jumped back up
when I realized I was lying on the same Raggedy Ann
bedspread that I'd slept under since I was four years old.
I ripped it off, then went to my mother's room and stole
her lavender spread. I draped it over my bed, even
though half of it ended up bunched on the floor.

I sat and looked around and tried to imagine Wesley
inside my room, the room in which I'd lately spent
hours practicing our first kiss in my mind. I looked at
the nightstand with my cheerleader romances in a tall
stack. I looked at the poster of the cast of *Buffy the*

Vampire Slayer on the wall. I looked at the orange-and-yellow flowered bag full of the makeup that had turned me into a raccoon.

All at once I felt ridiculous. I was as bad as Mom, casting Wesley as some kind of prince, all puckered up for a kiss. The *last* thing I wanted to do was kiss Wesley. The idea made me want to burst into tears right then and there.

At least Wesley knew nothing about my little trips into Fantasyland. And I didn't *have* to kiss him. I certainly would *not* kiss him. I wouldn't even *think* about it while he was there. We were going to finish our play and that was *all*.

I let out my breath, feeling much calmer. Then the doorbell rang.

I leapt to my feet and caught sight of myself in the mirror over my dresser. Pink splotches were spreading over my neck and cheeks. Should I ignore the bell, pretend I wasn't home?

"No, idiot," I told my reflection. Then I ran to the front door and yanked it open just to get the excruciating moment over with.

There was Wesley, looking red-eyed and deprived of sleep as usual. He wore a wrinkled plaid shirt buttoned up tight, also as usual. Only his hair looked different, smooth and flat, as if he'd actually combed it for once.

I motioned him to come inside. "My mom and brother are at the store. They'll be right back."

76

He nodded and cleared his throat.

"We could go in my room, if you want." As I turned to lead him into the hall, I tripped over a bump in the carpet. I walked the rest of the way into my room with my hands over my face.

Wesley stood awkwardly in the middle of my room, his eyes darting around as if they were afraid to land on anything.

"Go ahead, sit down," I said testily.

He obeyed like a trained dog, turning and sitting on the edge of my bed in one mechanical move.

"So . . . ," he began. Then he cleared his throat about five times.

"So . . . ," I prompted.

"So, I've been thinking about the end, and I really think it would compromise our theme if Steve doesn't die."

"Are you crazy?" I yelled, happy to dive back into arguing about the play. "The theme is not that love stinks, the theme is that love makes everything bearable."

He leaned back on his hands. "I don't see anything unbearable happening in the play, unless you count the part where Steve kisses Marcy's skirt."

I shot him a "don't start that again" look.

"What we need," he said, "is more pathos."

"No, we don't. We can't possibly need something I've never even heard of."

Wesley took a deep breath and launched into speech

mode. "Pathos is the sorrow that is life. It is the tragic element that underlies everything, even our most—"

I put up a hand to stop him. "Okay, how about this: Steve meets the pit bull and gets mangled, but he doesn't die. He just gets horribly disfigured."

Wesley's eyes lit up. "Now, that has possibilities."

"Yes, it's perfect!" I dropped beside him on the bed. "He's hideous, but Marcy sticks by his side anyway, because she loves him so much that she doesn't care what he looks like."

"That might work. It's still a tragedy, but not a senseless tragedy."

"Right. And that's how Steve discovers what Marcy knew all along: that love makes everything okay."

I turned to smile at Wesley and realized my leg was touching his. His thigh was harder with muscle than I would have thought, and warm. My smile slid away as he stared at me. His eyes moved down to fix on my lips. I could almost hear the word *kiss* like a whisper between us.

A giggle bubbled up into my throat. Then Wesley's gold-brown eyes moved back up to mine and I felt myself go still all over. Our faces drifted closer together. And then—

Bang! Something hit the wall of my room from the other side. Wesley and I jumped apart.

"Jeanette!" Bill's voice roared.

I groaned. Bill was drunk.

Wesley looked dazed. "Who's that?"

"My brother's dad."

We sat in frozen silence. Then Bill's voice came louder, closer. "Jeanette, you whore, where the hell are you?"

The ugly words echoed down the hall toward my room. I clapped my hands over my ears as if that could make them stop. I squeezed my eyes shut, too, unable to bear the look on Wesley's face. Then I felt him jump to his feet and had to open my eyes to grab his arm.

"Don't move," I whispered. "Just wait till he goes away."

Wesley jerked his arm away. "I'm going home." He pulled open the door at the same time Bill was moving past it toward my mother's room.

Bill turned and loomed before Wesley, glaring at him through slitted eyes. He clamped a hand on Wesley's shoulder. "Who the hell are you?"

Wesley's mouth opened and closed.

I ran at Bill and slugged his arm. "He's my friend. Leave him alone!"

That was when Mom came strolling down the hall. She stopped and put her hands on her hips. "Bill, what are you doing here? Who said you could come in?"

Bill let go of Wesley and turned on my mother. "There you are, whore. I saw you yesterday in front of the theater, kissing that football player. Everyone saw you."

My humiliation was physical, like nausea, and Wesley's was probably worse. I still couldn't make myself look at him, but I could feel his desperation to get out of my room. Bill was still blocking the doorway.

"Bill, will you please move?" I asked, my voice tight with tears.

"Everyone down at the bar is talking about it!" Bill shouted.

"It's really none of your business," said Mom coolly.

"The hell it isn't! You think I want my son—"

"Will you *move!*" I gave Bill a desperate shove. Luckily, he was drunk enough that he lost his balance and stumbled out of the way. Wesley and I bumped heads as we lurched out of my room.

I fled toward the front door with Wesley right behind me. It felt as if we were escaping together, and once we hit the cool air outside I turned to say, "I'm *so* sorry." But Wesley sprinted past me, down the driveway, past Bill's truck and onto the street.

I stood there alone with the sound of yelling voices behind me. I touched my dry lips.

Then Andrew came running up the driveway yelling, "Daddy! Daddy! Daddy's here!"

chapter eleven

Beware the Ides of March.

As I walked to school the morning of my birthday, Shakespeare's words kept repeating themselves in my head. It was wet outside, and gloomy. The cold made my body so stiff that it took a huge effort to put one foot in front of the other.

Or maybe it wasn't the cold that was slowing me down; maybe it was my despair over Wesley. The day before, we'd gone to the library at lunch and written furiously to finish our play on time. I didn't mention what had happened at my house and neither did he. We both knew that nothing we said would change anything. And we both knew that someone like me did not belong in his life. His family went to church. His mother was head of the PTA, his father the head of the U.S. Forest Service in Trinity County. Wesley was going to run for president. After hearing my drunk stepfather call my mother a whore, how could he not feel disgusted? How could he want anything to do with me? For his sake, I wished we could divide our play in half and turn it in separately so our names wouldn't have to appear together on the title page.

Of course, it was much too late for that, and when we handed Mrs. Gober the play, her eyebrows bobbed up and down. "I can't wait to read this one."

I offered Wesley a tentative smile but he only turned away and went to his desk.

A whole day later Wesley still hadn't spoken to me. I dragged myself into California history and sat, listless, as Doug asked Jake Bloom if he'd seen Stacey that morning and if he knew whether she'd gone anywhere the night before.

I sat, uninterested, as Mr. Reginald walked to the chalkboard and wrote "March 15th" before facing the class. "On this day in history, in 44 B.C., Julius Caesar was assassinated in Rome. Czar Nicholas the Second abdicated his throne in Russia on this date in 1917. This is also the day President Andrew Jackson and Teresa Dinsmore were born. Happy birthday, Teri."

I even sat, unmoved, when Doug leaned across the aisle and whispered, "Hey. Happy birthday."

"Thank you," I whispered back. But I still felt as empty as I'd felt since I watched Wesley running away from my house.

I dared to hope that Wesley might remember my birthday, and then he'd have to say *something* to me in biology. But he sat through the entire class at his desk in front of mine staring ahead as if I wasn't there.

When class was over, I stayed in my seat until everyone else was gone; then I got up and headed straight for the office. I didn't bother to fake being sick. I just walked out the front door of the office, right past Principal Holling and everyone, and walked home through the damp, oppressive air.

I expected Mom to demand an explanation of why I was home so early, but she was on the phone and didn't even glance at me as I flopped onto the couch.

"No!" she said, her voice choked with emotion. "Don't say that! ... No, that's not what I meant ... Nolan, please don't say that."

I picked up one of the throw pillows and pressed it over my face.

"Nolan ... baby," my mother pleaded. "I can't stand this, I can't ... Nolan, don't hang up!" She banged down the phone and gave a panicked sob.

I moved the pillow off my face. "Mom? You okay?"

She twisted around to look at me. "No," she said hoarsely. "I'm not."

"What happened?"

"It's Nolan. He ... We had a fight, a horrible fight." She sprang from her chair. "I have to go see him. I can't let it end like this."

She grabbed her purse off the coffee table and went to the hall closet for her coat. I followed.

"Mom!" I could hear the whine in my voice. "You're going to Redding now? Today?"

Mom jammed her arm into her sleeve. "Honey, I have to. Nolan is everything to me. I can't lose him."

"But, Mom—"

"Please, Teresa. I have to go." She stooped in front of the hall mirror and wiped the tears from her face. She fluffed her blond bangs, her bracelets clacking. Then she pressed a kiss to the side of my head and was out the door.

I stood, staring at the closed door in slow shock. A few moments later Mom opened the door and stepped inside. I put my hand to my heart in relief. She'd finally remembered it was my birthday.

"I can't believe I almost forgot," she said. "Andrew's not going to After Care today. The bus will be dropping him off in about an hour. Would you be a lifesaver and keep an eye on him? Thanks, sweetie."

I watched out the window as she drove her Toyota onto the street. Then I turned and walked to my room. I sank onto the bed and tilted slowly down sideways until my cheek touched the mattress. I cried a little. Then I just lay there, empty again.

"What's wrong with you?" Andrew asked an hour later from my doorway.

I considered telling him, "It's my birthday and no one cares." But I would have felt pathetic trying to milk sympathy from a five-year-old.

"I'm just having a bad day," I said. "Go watch TV."

Andrew didn't argue. I stayed in my room with the

door open, listening as Elmer Fudd tried to murder Bugs Bunny. I finally fell asleep out of boredom.

When I woke, it was dark and Gramma was sitting at the foot of my bed. She patted my leg and said, "Happy birthday, Teri." I sat up to lean into her hug. She patted my back while I rested my cheek on her shoulder and breathed in the scent of talc and Avon lotion.

Gramma stood and tugged on my hand. "Up you go. I have something to show you."

The rest of the house was dark, too, and before we got to the living room I could hear Andrew giggling. Then we turned the corner and there on the coffee table was a yellow cake that glowed with burning candles.

Gramma and Andrew sang "Happy Birthday to You" and clapped when they were through. I kneeled in front of the cake and felt the warmth of the candles reach toward my face.

"Make a wish," Gramma said.

I thought, My wishes never come true, why bother? I blew out the candles.

While Gramma cut the cake, Andrew hopped around saying, "Cake, cake, yum!" Then we all sat down on the couch to eat cake and lick frosting from our fingers.

While we were still eating, Samantha came in, hunched inside Brian's too-big army coat, her eyes hidden under the brim of her cap. She looked from the candles to me, then said, "Oh. Happy birthday." Her eyes were glassy, a sure sign she'd been smoking pot. She sat down beside Andrew with a piece of cake and ate it slowly. "This is the best cake I've ever tasted," she said.

Andrew brought me a piece of folded construction paper smeared with frosting. "I made you a birthday card."

"Oh. Thank you." I opened the card. Inside was a crayon picture of a happy face with Andrew's name scrawled in lopsided letters. I hugged him and ended up with frosting in my hair. Next, Gramma gave me her present, the same one she gives each of us every year: a certificate for a free haircut at her salon. Then she gave Samantha a sharp poke.

Samantha looked at me and shrugged. "You could have my purple sweater, I guess."

I mumbled another thank-you. I'd been drooling over Samantha's purple sweater for the past year and whenever I asked to borrow it, I always got a loud "No!" But at that moment, it didn't matter that the sweater was now mine.

It didn't even help when the phone rang and Mom's voice shouted "Happy birthday!" into my ear. She said she was sorry, sorry, *so* sorry it had slipped her mind, and I just had to forgive her. She said she'd make it up to me tomorrow, she'd take me to dinner, just the two of us. She said she was sorry but she just didn't have the energy to drive back home that night, but the trip had been worth it because she and Nolan had made up. And oh yes, Nolan sent his love and she probably shouldn't spoil the surprise, but Nolan was going to give me a hundred dollars to buy myself the biggest, best birthday present ever, wasn't that nice?

After I hung up, Gramma asked, "Is she on her way home?"

When I shook my head, Gramma's lips pressed together, but she didn't say a word. Part of me wished she'd call Mom up and make her come home. But part of me was glad she hadn't said anything. Why make it more obvious that my mother didn't want to be with me on my birthday?

"I thought I'd treat you kids to pizza for dinner," Gramma said. "I can drive you down to pick it up, but then I have to head home and feed some hungry kitties."

Samantha called in the pizza order and they all got on their coats. "Teri," Gramma called. "You coming?"

I shook my head. She gave me one of her long, blank looks. Then she turned to follow Andrew and Samantha out the door.

I sat alone in the quiet living room. I already hated being fifteen.

I gazed down at my leftover cake. I regretted not having made a wish. If I had wished for Wesley to kiss me, it might have happened eventually.

There was still half a cake left. I dropped to my knees and stabbed the candles back into the cake. I ran into the kitchen to get a box of matches out of the jar on top of the refrigerator, the only spot in the house Andrew couldn't reach yet. I used three matches to light the candles and tossed the rest onto the table. I closed my eyes.

"I wish for Wesley to kiss me," I said out loud. Then I blew out the candles all in one breath.

I should have gone straight back to the kitchen and put the matches back in the jar. I've asked myself a hundred times why I didn't. Why did I just sit there until Samantha and Andrew came home with the pizza, filling the house with the smell of pepperoni? Why didn't I grab the matches as I followed Samantha into the kitchen to get a plate? Why didn't I notice them on the coffee table when I was sprawled on the couch with Andrew and Samantha, watching Nick at Nite?

Samantha actually didn't watch TV for very long. After about ten minutes, she lurched to her feet and said, "I've got to go to sleep."

Even though it was Andrew's bedtime, I let him stay up late to keep me company while I watched *The Brady Bunch*. When it was over I clicked the TV off with the remote and told Andrew he had to go to bed.

"But I'm not sleepy," Andrew whined.

"Well, I am."

Andrew grabbed on to the couch cushion. "I want to stay up."

I pried him off the couch, dragged him to his room and tossed him on his bed. "Go to sleep!" I went into the bathroom to wash my face and brush my teeth. Just in case my birthday wish came true, I couldn't let myself get too lazy about hygiene. Feeling very adult, I walked around the house to make sure all the doors and windows were locked and the heat was turned down.

Samantha was snoring as I slipped on the extra-large Scooby-Doo T-shirt I slept in. I crawled into bed and twisted around, trying to find a comfortable position.

I was half asleep when I remembered the matches again. I thought, I better get up and put them away. And it seemed to me that I really was getting up. It seemed to me that I really was picking up the matches from the coffee table and carrying them into the kitchen.

Now I know it was just a dream. But I can still remember it, clear as day. I remember how my hand reached up and up to the jar on top of the refrigerator. And I remember the red and black triangles on the box of matches, and how they looked, tumbling down, down, into the jar.

chapter
twelve

The smoke alarm filtered into my dream. Me and Wesley were somewhere in ancient Rome, watching a bunch of Roman senators in togas act out our play. Julius Caesar ran by, yelling, "Beware the Ides of March! Beware the Ides of March!" Then an alarm sounded and Wesley said, "Oh, a fire drill," before he got up and walked out without me.

When I finally woke, the loud *beep-beep-beep* startled me so much that I jumped up and staggered across the room with my hands over my ears. I hit the light and for a moment I thought there was something wrong with my eyes. The entire room was dimmed by a gray film. Then I smelled it. Smoke.

Adrenaline slammed through my body, and I leapt onto Samantha's bed to shake her awake. I pulled her half off the mattress, shrieking, "Smoke! Smoke!"

Samantha struggled to her feet and looked wildly around. "What? Christ, that noise!"

"Smoke!" I cried. "Something's on fire!"

We gripped each other's arms, our eyes locked in terror. Then Samantha whispered, "Andrew."

My sister flew to the door. I knew from my Junior Fireman book that you're supposed to touch the top of the door first to make sure it's not hot, but before I could say anything Samantha had already ripped open the door and run out into the hall.

I stumbled out after her, but the smoke was so much thicker out there, I couldn't see her. Tears flooded my stinging eyes and my next breath hurt. I dropped to my hands and knees, another Junior Fireman rule. I couldn't breathe any easier, but I yelled to Samantha, "Hands and knees!"

I crawled, coughing and crying, down the hall until I saw the smoke pouring out of Andrew's open doorway. I froze in horror. Oh, no, the matches. I'd left the matches out, and Andrew had got them, and now he was dead and it was all my fault!

Then Samantha plunged out of Andrew's room, hauling him with her. He was limp. I screamed, certain he was dead. Andrew coughed and I rushed to him, hysterical sounds squeezing through my raw throat.

"Come on!" Samantha yelled. "Hurry!"

We dragged Andrew through the living room. Samantha fumbled with the lock on the front door and all at once we fell out the door into the sweet, cold air. We ran together across the grass with Andrew shrieking and coughing and kicking all at the same time.

At the street Samantha let go of Andrew and stopped to turn around, gripping her side. She stared at the house, saying, "Son of a bitch! Son of a bitch!"

I eased Andrew onto the asphalt of the beauty salon's parking lot, then huddled up close to Samantha to look at the house. All I could see was the light from our bedroom window. "I don't see any fire," I said.

"You will," said Samantha. "Half of Andrew's room is blazing. The little moron was trying to put it out with his squirt gun."

We stood, gazing stupidly at the house. Andrew was doing less coughing and more crying. I began to shiver from the cold.

"Son of a bitch! We didn't call the fire department." Samantha started back to the house, but I grabbed her shirt. "No! You can't go back in there!"

"It's okay." She pushed my hands away. "The fire's not near the phone."

"But the smoke!" I clung to her with a crazed strength. "You could pass out from the smoke! Don't go back in!"

"Do you want the whole house to burn down?" Samantha demanded.

"You can't go back in!"

"All right! Then run over to Old Man Harrelson's and call 911."

"No! If I leave, you might go back in!"

"Fine!" Samantha yelled, shaking me loose. "I'll go call myself. Stay here and watch Andrew!"

Samantha ran to Mr. Harrelson's house and I heard her banging on his front door as I kneeled beside Andrew.

"Mommy, Mommy, Mommy," he cried over and over. It was even colder than I'd thought. Frost sparkled on the concrete around us. My hands and feet already hurt from the cold. I pulled Andrew onto my lap as much for warmth as to comfort him.

By the time Samantha came running back wearing Mr. Harrelson's coat, a shifting orange light glowed from the left side of the house. By the time we heard the first wail of the fire trucks, flames darted out of the wall and licked at the roof.

The blast of fire engines pulling up in front of our house finally scared Andrew silent. One of the firemen saw me and Andrew pressed back against the side of the beauty salon and pointed us out to Mr. Harrelson, who had met the fire trucks in his robe and slippers.

Mr. Harrelson's white hair waved over his head in a gust of wind as he walked toward us. He pulled us against his sides and hurried us toward his house.

"Where's Samantha?" I shouted to him.

"She's fine," he said. "Come inside now."

Mrs. Harrelson gathered us in at the door and snapped at her husband, "Get the hose out and wet down that fence before it catches, too!"

Mrs. Harrelson hustled me and Andrew to a couch and tossed several blankets on us, then crossed to the window to stare anxiously out. Her face shone with night cream and her hair lay trapped under a pink hair net. The red lights from the fire trucks swept across her face and threw her shadow intermittently into our laps. I heard the shouts of men outside and the splatter of water from the fire hoses.

I wanted to stand next to Mrs. Harrelson and watch out the window, too, but I was too cold to move. Andrew must have been in shock, because he just sat there, clutching the blanket as he coughed hoarsely. His eyes were like dark holes in his white face.

A banging at the front door made me jump. Mrs. Harrelson gasped and put her hand to her heart as she rushed to open the door. The paramedics had come to take us to the hospital.

One paramedic, dressed all in white, leaned over me and his fingers were cold on my wrist. Even his coat was cold as it brushed against my arm.

"Have you got anything we can put on their feet?" the other paramedic asked as he checked Andrew's pulse.

Mrs. Harrelson rushed into a bedroom and came back with two thick pairs of socks. I gratefully pulled mine over my frozen feet. The paramedics wrapped scratchy blankets around our shoulders and started us out the door. That was when Gramma came rushing up the walk with a scarf flapping around her head and her regular shoes on beneath her pajamas.

Gramma touched my face, then kneeled before Andrew and scooped him in for a hug. He started crying again and when Gramma leaned back from him, a string of spit clung to her shoulder and stretched to his mouth. Samantha was already sitting in the back of the ambulance, and while Gramma helped Andrew up inside, I looked back over my shoulder. Our house was nothing but a fiery outline against the black sky. Orange embers flew up in a wild swirl, then came down in a shower of ashes. As I turned back to the ambulance, the ashes drifted gently against my face.

chapter
thirteen

In the emergency room, they left me lying alone on a stretcher behind a curtain while they examined Andrew in a cubicle nearby. Tense words passed back and forth over the sound of Andrew's hoarse crying before they whisked him away to take him "upstairs."

I sat up. "Is Andrew okay?" I called. But no one was left to hear me.

I lay back down to wait. I waited forever with nothing to do but worry and breathe in my own smoky smell. Why didn't someone come back and tell me what was wrong with Andrew? Had they forgotten me?

Then came footsteps and a hand ripping the curtain aside. Mom stood there, looking at me from a ravaged face.

I burst into tears. Mom stumbled forward to crush me in a hug.

As I pressed my face into her shoulder, I saw Nolan lurking behind her. Like an actor who had wandered onto the wrong set, he was gazing at the medical equipment pushed up against the wall.

I pulled back. "What's *he* doing here?"

"Oh, honey," said Mom as she stroked my hair. "He's concerned for you, of course."

I didn't care. I didn't want him watching me cry. He must have figured that out, because he began backing away and pointing over to the waiting room.

"I'll just be over there, Jeanette," he said. "If you need anything."

As soon as he was out of sight, I blurted out, "The fire! It was all my fault! I left the matches out. I left them on the coffee table and Andrew got them, and it's all my fault!"

Mom put her arms around me and tucked my head under her chin. "It's okay. Nothing matters except that my sweet babies are okay."

That only made me cry harder. "B-but Andrew!" I sobbed. "I don't think—he's not okay!"

Mom's fingers dug into my arms. *"What do you mean? Where's Andrew?"*

I pointed upstairs. Mom took off for the elevator. I was right behind her.

We found Andrew lying in a small room with an oxygen mask strapped to his face. As Mom moved toward the bed, her legs buckled and she had to grab on to a chair to hold herself up. I didn't know what was worse, seeing Andrew hooked up to a machine to help him breathe, or seeing the way Mom's hands trembled as she stroked his hair.

A doctor in a green medical suit came in and huddled with Mom and Gramma and Samantha. He talked in a half-whisper about smoke inhalation and what they had to do to "repair" Andrew's lungs. He said chances were good for a quick recovery, but added, "Only time will tell how bad the damage is."

I pressed myself into the corner of the room, my arms flat against the cool wall. This is all *my fault,* I thought. Why doesn't someone scream at me?

Eventually, I realized that no one was screaming at me because they were all too busy trying to take the blame for themselves. Mom insisted it was all her fault for deciding to spend the night in Redding. "It was your birthday," she said to me in a pained whisper. "I should have been home and I wasn't, and you all could have *died...."*

Gramma believed she was the one at fault. She was the one who had brought over the cake and candles and hadn't made sure the matches were out of reach before she'd gone home. Samantha also claimed fault, because she was the oldest, she'd been in charge and she should have known better than to go to bed before Andrew was asleep. Even Nolan took some blame, telling us he shouldn't have asked Mom to stay the night at his house.

We were like the Greek chorus in our very own tragedy, with chants of *my fault, my fault* layered together throughout the night. I thought about calling Wesley and telling him that I finally understood what *pathos* meant.

I didn't call him, of course. I didn't leave Andrew's room the entire night. I just sat by his bed with Mom and Gramma and Samantha while Nolan brought us cup after cup of vending machine hot chocolate. None of us could stop saying we were sorry.

The day after the fire, I went with Mom and Samantha to see how bad the damage was. Samantha and I both agreed the fire department had arrived so quickly that there was a good chance most of the house was okay. As we drove over from the hospital, Mom and Samantha said things like "I hope my CDs made it" and "I hope the photo albums didn't catch."

Then we pulled up in front of the burned house. My mother shut off the car. We sat in silence, trying to make ourselves believe what we were seeing. The entire left side of the house was a black, hollowed-out shell that looked ready to disintegrate. The living room windows were gaping holes with black stains around them. Most of the shrubs and bushes in the flower beds were singed black, too. The front door was still white, though, with a few dark smudges left by the firemen passing through.

We slowly got out of the car, our eyes riveted to the house. We didn't notice Edna Porter walking toward us across the beauty salon parking lot until she called out, "Jeanette Brungard!"

Mom turned her head slowly, like a sleepwalker. Mrs. Porter was ancient, and she looked small and frail as she shuffled toward us. But her voice was sharp as she barked, "Jeanette! There's a sign on the shop door that says 'Closed until Monday.'"

"Is there?" Mom said.

Mrs. Porter locked her purse beneath her elbow as she shook a gnarled finger at Mom. "I had an appointment this morning at ten o'clock for a wash and set."

"Oh?" asked my mother, her eyes inching back to the house.

"Yes, I did. If your mother was going to close shop, the least she could have done was cancel her appointments and not let people come all the way down here to find out!"

Samantha put her hand to her head, which looked strangely naked without her baseball cap. "Mrs. Porter! Just look at our house!"

"Yes, I saw it. A terrible shame. Jeanette, you tell your mother if she wants to keep her customers she'd better have a little consideration."

As Mrs. Porter marched away on her stiff legs, we were already moving up the walk to our house.

Mom began to breathe hard and fast as she opened the front door. Even Samantha gasped as she stepped through the doorway. But when I walked into the living room behind her, all my emotions seemed to fall out of me and scurry back outside to wait. I didn't feel anything at all. I was like a video camera, recording everything to put together later.

I'd expected everything to be dry and powdery black, like a cold fireplace, but everything was wet, drenched by the fire hoses. The carpet squished beneath our feet as we walked, leaving puddles of black water in the shape of our footprints. Water dripped from the blackened ceiling and made streaks down black walls that had been peach-colored just the day before. Only half of the living room was actually burned, but the other half was ruined by water and soot, and it was full of the dirty smell of wet ashes.

We went down the hall and saw right away that all the bedrooms had caught fire. Andrew's room was the worst: nothing left but charred ceiling beams and the curly metal springs of his mattress. Even the wall that separated his room from my mother's was gone, and we could see straight to the toilet sitting open in her bathroom. The furniture in her room looked as if it had been boiled down and painted black. The vanity had completely disappeared into a pile of charred splinters.

Mom dug around in her closet, pushing aside the remnants of her clothes, poking through the ash heaps that were once boxes.

"My pictures. My diaries," she said, the first thing she'd said since we got there. She dug through the soggy pile faster, bent over, like a dog searching for a buried bone. "They're all gone, there's nothing left." She stood and covered her face with her sooty hands while she cried. "My whole life, it's all gone!"

I turned away. Nothing in that house had really been mine; it had all belonged to my mother. Sure, I had my clothes, but except for my Irish sweater and a few other things, they were all hand-me-downs from Samantha, and they were getting too small for me anyway. The only things that were truly mine were the makeup bag Mom had given me and a few stuffed animals and other toys in the back of my closet that I hadn't played with in years. Oh, and a stack of romance novels that I'd already read.

I felt bad that I didn't feel worse, so I left Mom and Samantha combing through the bedrooms and went into the kitchen. Everything in the kitchen was covered with ashes and stained by smoke and water, but nothing had caught fire. Plates were still stacked in the sink and clumped with frosting from my birthday cake. A pan of dried spaghetti sauce sat on the stove. The jar meant to keep matches away from Andrew still sat on top of the refrigerator. I opened the freezer and looked at the stacks of Swanson TV dinners. I poked a package of hamburger. It was still mostly frozen.

I heard a voice from the living room call, "Hello!" and went in to see who it was.

A woman I vaguely recognized stood in the doorway with two black-haired kids around eight or nine.

"Yeah?" I said.

The woman looked gravely at me and talked in a low, serious voice, as if she was at a funeral. "I'm so sorry to disturb you at a time like this. But I just couldn't pass up the opportunity to show my children the terrible consequences of fire. Would you mind if I let them come in and look?"

I stared at her in dull surprise. "Um, I guess not."

"Thank you so very much," the woman said. She grabbed her children's hands and tugged them inside. All three stood in the middle of the wet, dark living room, their heads swiveling around.

"You see?" the mother whispered to her kids. "You see why I tell you to never, ever play with fire?"

The older kid, a boy, stretched his neck to see down the hall. The girl stared only at me.

"Well," said the woman to me, "I wish better luck for you and your family." Then she pulled her children out the door. I followed them out and stood in the front yard to watch them get into their minivan. I watched the woman strap seat belts onto the kids, then watched her get into her car and turn on her blinker before pulling onto the street and driving away.

I turned toward my house again and my eyes moved up the bare limbs of the giant oak that stretched over the roof of our house. I would never again hear acorns thudding to the roof with each September breeze. I would never again sit in front of my mother's magic mirror while she braided my hair. I would never again look out the front window and wave to Gramma as she closed down the beauty shop for the day. And I would never again chase Andrew down the hall to his room, yelling, "Tickle! Tickle!"

My emotions fell back into me so quick and hard that I dropped down to my knees. I dug my fingers into the brown, dead grass, and tears squeezed from my eyes for the first time since the fire. Still, even though I felt sad, my crying felt insincere, as if I was performing for an unseen audience. I stopped and got to my feet, then walked slowly to the car to wait for my mother and sister.

That night we slept at Gramma's trailer. Even though I was more tired than I'd ever been in my life, I had a hard time falling asleep.

For one thing, there was only one double bed in Gramma's spare bedroom, so Samantha and I had to share, and she practically took up the whole bed. For another thing, I couldn't seem to get the smell of smoke out of my head. I'd start to drift away, then I'd find myself sitting up just to breathe.

Even when I finally did fall asleep, I kept smelling the smoke, and I found myself running around my house, trying to find the fire. Then somehow the fire was everywhere, all around me, burning away the walls and even the floor beneath me. Then the flames completely swallowed up the floor and I fell into thin air.

I was falling from the fire with nothing but terrifying blackness beneath me. I opened my mouth to scream when my body jerked me awake and I rose up into the dark of Gramma's spare bedroom, gasping for air.

Samantha turned over with a groan. "Christ, what is your *problem*?"

I pressed my hand against my chest, trying to slow my racing heartbeat. "I don't know. I keep thinking I smell smoke."

She was quiet for a long moment. "Yeah," she said as she rolled back toward the wall. "Me too."

I lay back down. I hoped the smoke smell would leave my head soon. I hoped it wasn't stuck there forever.

chapter
fourteen

Spring break started only a few days after the fire, which meant I didn't have to go back to school for nearly two weeks. During that time all the churches in town collected about twenty boxes of clothes for our family, so I had a whole new wardrobe that was a lot more interesting than the one I'd lost. Each time I went into a store I saw a jar or a coffee can near the cash register with a sign that said DONATIONS FOR THE RICKMAN FAMILY. I don't know why they said Rickman, because Andrew was the only one with that last name.

Mom said the donations were over a thousand dollars, which I thought was an amazing amount. But Mom's voice was bitter as she said, "That won't even begin to buy my life back."

Gramma said Mom shouldn't worry so much, the house was insured and they'd be getting a big check from the insurance company soon. But that didn't make Mom feel better.

"Sure," she said. "You'll build a new house, but I still lost everything that belonged to *me*."

See, it was always Gramma's house. She bought it with the insurance money she got when Grampa died in the mailbox accident. When my mother and father got married, Gramma offered to let them live there for only $150 a month to cover taxes and insurance. After my father took off for Texas, Mom stayed in the house with Gramma's blessing. No matter how many times Mom got married and divorced, she couldn't afford to leave a $150-a-month three-bedroom house.

The day after the fire Mom said, "It's no use looking for another place to rent; you know we can't afford it."

Still, we all figured she had to get around to it eventually. Gramma's trailer had three bedrooms, but it was still a trailer and the rooms were all tiny. The living room had only space enough for Gramma's rocking chair and a love seat, so there wasn't even room for all of us to sit and watch TV. Not that there was much to watch. Gramma didn't have cable and got only two fuzzy stations through the antenna.

With all of us tripping over each other, Samantha would last until about noon before she took off for the hardware store to wait for Brian to get off work. Meanwhile, with no TV and no toys, Andrew's only entertainment was to try to catch one of Gramma's three cats, even though he was supposed to stay quiet, and recover. If he managed to catch one, he'd carry it around in a death grip until it fought its way free. After only a few days, his arms were covered with thin red scratches.

As for me, I'd get so stir-crazy that I didn't even mind when Mom ordered me to take Andrew to the park or to the library. "For the love of God, get him out of here," she'd say. "I can't even hear myself think!"

I'd stay gone as long as possible, hoping that would help Mom think her way toward renting us a new place. As soon as we got back to the trailer, I'd go looking for her, my fingers crossed that I'd find her reading the classified ads or making calls. But mostly I'd find her at the kitchen table, staring into a cup of coffee grown cold.

Gramma said Mom needed time to mourn everything she'd lost. She said it was normal for Mom to do nothing but mope around the trailer in Gramma's frilly bathrobe without bothering to take a shower. But seeing Mom without makeup was as weird as seeing Samantha without her baseball cap. I barely recognized her. And Samantha and I had no idea how to act around her. If one of us mentioned something we'd lost in the fire, she'd collapse into tears. Yet if Andrew cried about something he'd lost, she'd yell at him. I was almost glad when she finally took off to Redding to spend the night at Nolan's.

Andrew wasn't glad, though. He stood at the window, staring at the empty street for a long time. Then he came to me, picked up my hand and pulled me to the phone. "I want to call my daddy."

About an hour later, Bill showed up at the trailer and said he was taking Andrew home with him.

Gramma said, "Over my dead body."

But Andrew clung to Bill's leg. "I want to go to Daddy's house. I want to stay with my daddy."

I didn't blame Andrew much. Still, as I watched him out the front window, struggling to haul himself up into Bill's truck, I felt unexpected tears fill my eyes.

As soon as Bill pulled away, Gramma picked up the phone and called my mother at Nolan's.

"Your son has just been snatched out from under your nose," she said into the phone. Then, "You mean you're going to let that man get away with kidnapping?"

Gramma bowed her head and lightly touched the bridge of her nose. "Because I thought you might be concerned. I see I was mistaken."

After she hung up, she turned away from the phone, her face more carefully blank than ever. "I don't know what's wrong with your mother. I could just turn her over my knee." It was the strongest thing I'd ever heard her say against Mom.

On Easter Sunday we got a lot of invitations to attend different church services.

"Can't we go to at least one?" I asked Gramma as she scooped grounds into her coffeemaker. "Just one church, just this one time?"

She frowned down into the coffee can. "What on earth for?"

"Just to see what it's like. Find out stuff about God."

"I know all I care to know about God." She snapped the plastic cover back onto the can. "And I have no use for a god that would allow a patch of ice to kill a good man."

Later, when Mom arrived with Nolan, all dressed up for Easter dinner at Nolan's mother's house, I asked if she'd go with me.

"All those churches, they gave us all those boxes of clothes," I added. "Don't you think we should—"

"Excuse me," Mom said from the swaying rocker, "but I don't think I'll be joining the forces of hypocrisy today, thank you very much."

"Amen to that," said Nolan before giving the antenna on the TV another twist.

So instead of going to church, we sat around in the tiny living room while Nolan finished watching a hockey game through the fuzzy reception.

At five minutes to noon, Samantha and I piled into Gramma's car to follow Mom and Nolan up Harper's Hill to Mrs. Redmond's house. As soon as we arrived, Mrs. Redmond put Samantha to work peeling potatoes in her big country kitchen and ordered me to help Mom and Nolan set the table in the dining room.

"And you, Dorinda," said Mrs. Redmond from where she was rolling out biscuit dough on the counter. "You have such a way with sauces, would you mind taking charge of the raisin sauce?"

"Not at all," Gramma said, and tied on an apron.

Even with Samantha sitting two feet away swiping at

potatoes and me at her elbow pulling silverware from a drawer, Mrs. Redmond didn't seem at all uncomfortable talking about Mom.

"It's not that I don't like Jeanette," she said to Gramma. "I've always said no one sets a better permanent than Jeanette Rickman. But—"

"Brungard," Gramma corrected. "It's Jeanette Brungard."

"Yes, well, my point is—and I think you'll agree with me—that she is much too accommodating. I don't believe it's healthy for Nolan to be encouraged in his whims. I believe he needs to be encouraged to take on real responsibility. It's high time he started a family of his own...."

I left the kitchen, arms loaded, and found Mom and Nolan kicked back at the dining room table, drinking wine. Mom's bare feet were in Nolan's lap.

Mom waved a hand toward the kitchen. "They're talking about us, aren't they? What are they saying?"

I set the silverware down. "Who?"

"The unholy alliance in there," Nolan said.

Mom cracked up. "Poor Nolan. I thought *I* had a controlling mother. You should hear what *he's* had to put up with."

I went back into the kitchen for glasses. Samantha gave me her "do me a favor and kill me now" look.

"And," Gramma said as she stirred the sauce with quick hard strokes, "you are also right that Nolan is entirely too irresponsible, and not at all the appropriate partner for a woman with three children to raise."

Mrs. Redmond pounded her biscuit dough so hard that her pearls began to swing back and forth from her neck. "I assume you do not mean to suggest that Nolan won't do an excellent job of raising children of his own."

"Of course not," said Gramma. "I hope he has a baker's dozen. With someone else."

I went back into the dining room, carefully balancing four glasses. Mom was still laughing, one hand clutching Nolan's sleeve, the other hand waving back and forth as if she couldn't take any more.

Nolan grabbed her hand and leaned closer to her. "And she hasn't even noticed that in all my books, the football player's mother always shows up at the wrong time and dies a gruesome death at the hands of the killer."

Mom screamed with laughter, slapping at his chest. "Stop, stop! I can't stand it!"

The door from the kitchen swung open and Mrs. Redmond stepped in. Mom's laughter squawked to an abrupt end as she took her feet from Nolan's lap and sat up straight. Mrs. Redmond coolly arched her penciled brow.

Nolan stood up and cleared his throat, seeming more like a little boy than a two-hundred-pound man with shoulders a mile wide. "Um, where did you say that tablecloth was?"

Half an hour later, we were all sitting around the table, eating scalloped potatoes and ham with Gramma's raisin sauce. Nolan had fallen completely silent, and Mom kept giving him nervous looks.

"Are you okay?" she finally whispered to him.

"Don't mind him," Mrs. Redmond said. "Nolan often pouts at the dinner table. Or hadn't you noticed?"

Mom stared down at her plate, nostrils flaring. Mrs. Redmond gazed at her expectantly, then smiled condescendingly when Mom didn't say anything.

Mrs. Redmond turned to ask me and Samantha about the night of the fire. She wanted to hear how we got Andrew out of the house.

"Good heavens," she said at the end of our story. "I hope you have all said a prayer of thanks to the good Lord for sparing your lives."

Samantha leaned toward Mrs. Redmond and in a confiding tone said, "Oh, we say tons of prayers. At least ten a day."

Gramma chose that moment to ask Mom why she hadn't picked up Andrew on the way over. "He should be here with us, especially today."

Mom sighed. "Mother, we've been over this and over this. Bill loves Andrew, and Andrew loves Bill. They're fine."

"Do you honestly believe that? With the way he drinks?"

"Mother, please!"

Then Samantha had to throw her two cents in. "You know what I think? I think you're unconsciously mad at Andrew for starting the fire."

"No!" my mother cried in a betrayed voice. "That's not true! How can you say such a thing! I'm not angry at Andrew, I'm angry at *me*. For being in Redding with Nolan when I should have been home with my children."

"Come now, Jeanette," said Mrs. Redmond. "You can hardly lay the blame on Nolan. You've never been one to stay home with your children. The chances were excellent that if ever there was a fire, you wouldn't be home."

In the awful silence that followed, Mom's color drained away. Gramma's face turned red, even though she didn't change her expression. Meanwhile, Samantha's mouth hung open and let out little bursts of shocked laughter.

Nolan threw his napkin down on the table. "You just don't know when to quit, do you?"

Mrs. Redmond smiled blandly. "My dear son, surely you know I'm not saying anything that half the town hasn't said already."

Mom began slipping down in her chair, curling in on herself and crossing her arms over her face. She looked like she was dying.

I jumped up from my chair and yelled, "Mommy!" I started around the table toward her, but Nolan had already pulled her to her feet and was half carrying her toward the kitchen.

"Look, Mom," he demanded. "Do you see the effect you have on people? Do you see?" Then he pushed the kitchen door open with his foot, swept my mother through the doorway and kicked the door shut behind them.

Gramma began folding her napkin in jerky mechanical moves. "Your hospitality is not what it used to be, Helen."

"Point taken." Mrs. Redmond took a sip from her water glass. "I will apologize for my timing, but not for what I said."

"No?" Gramma placed her fork across her plate. "She's lost everything already. And you see no reason not to add insult to injury?"

They were arguing in such civil tones that I wanted to scream. Why wasn't anyone defending Mom? Why wasn't anyone telling Mrs. Redmond she was wrong?

I looked at Samantha, but she just sat there with a stupid smirk as if she was enjoying the whole thing.

"Samantha!" I shouted across the table. "Tell her how old you are." But when Samantha said nothing, I repeated to Mrs. Redmond what I'd heard Mom tell one of the policemen who'd questioned her in Andrew's hospital room the night of the fire. "She's *eighteen*. She's a legal *adult*. There was an *adult* in the house when it caught fire."

Mrs. Redmond turned toward me and the corners of her mouth turned down in a look of pity. "Oh, you poor sweet girl. That's completely beside the point."

I looked at Mrs. Redmond—with her gray hair in a

stiff stack of curls that Mom had sprayed into place the day before—and I had to fight the urge to pick up a glass and fling it to the floor.

Gramma stood and pushed her own chair in. "I'm sure you'll understand if we don't stay."

"Now, Dorinda, there's no reason to blow this out of proportion," Mrs. Redmond began, but Gramma was already marching toward the kitchen. Samantha hopped up to follow her with a cheery "Thanks for dinner! It's been real!"

I joined the parade toward the door and we all walked out, leaving Mrs. Redmond alone in her dining room with our plates still half full of food.

Once in the kitchen, we found Nolan had already loaded Mom into his silver BMW. As we came down the back porch, he was walking around the front of his car to the driver's side.

"She's in pretty rough shape," he called to Gramma. "I'd better take her home."

"Whose home?" Gramma asked. "Yours or hers?"

Nolan lifted his hands, then got into his car without answering. As he started the engine, I ran toward the passenger door, yelling, "Mom! Mom!" But Mom's head was down and her hair covered her face and she didn't look up as Nolan backed out of the driveway.

Samantha stood beside me as we watched Nolan's car disappear down the winding road.

"She must not have heard me," I said.

Samantha snorted. "Yeah, right."

I gave her a halfhearted punch in the arm. She tapped me back before she walked off to Gramma's car.

On the way home, Gramma kept shaking her head and sighing. I held on to my stomach and thought, I will never eat raisin sauce again.

Then Samantha piped up with a "Hey! If Mom and the Hulk ever get married, just think how fun Christmas will be!"

I landed another punch on her shoulder. This time, she didn't bother trying to hit me back.

Mom spent the night at Nolan's and she came home early the next morning only to pick up her things before heading back to Redding. She told us she needed time to think. She said she didn't feel up to working in the beauty shop for a while. She said that after what Nolan's mother had said, she felt like the whole town was against her.

I sat in Gramma's rocking chair with a bowl of Honey Nut Cheerios, pretending I was watching *Good Morning America* instead of listening to Mom and Gramma argue in the kitchen.

"You're going to let a busybody like Helen Redmond make you turn tail and leave town?" Gramma asked.

"It's only for a few days," Mom said in an exasperated voice. "Is it all right with you if I take a few days to figure things out?"

"Why are you asking me? Why don't you ask your children?"

"Oh, so now you're judging me, too?" Mom cried. "Are you going to tell me what a lousy mother I am, too?"

"You're not the only one who's having a difficult time right now. Your children—"

"Okay, fine! If I ask them, will you let me be?"

Mom appeared in the doorway from the kitchen. "Teri, is it all right with you if I spend a few days at Nolan's?"

Her voice wobbled and her knuckles were white with her grip on the doorjamb. She looked like she was barely holding herself up. She looked as if she might go sliding down to the floor at any minute, falling in on herself like she had the day before.

I looked down at the brown carpet. "It's okay with me."

Mom made a small noise, which I supposed meant thank you, then threw open the door of the spare bedroom, where Samantha was still sleeping.

Mom once again demanded to know whether it was okay for her to spend a few days at Nolan's. Samantha groaned. "Why should I care?"

Mom shut the door, then came back into the living room. Gramma now stood by the front window, staring out.

"Are you satisfied, Mother? My children have given me their permission. May I go now?"

Gramma didn't say anything. A few minutes later, Mom was gone and Gramma and I were left alone with the sound of the TV, which seemed suddenly too loud. I put down my cereal bowl and picked up the remote to click the TV off.

"So," I said. "When do you think she'll come back?"

With a sigh, Gramma turned toward me. "I don't know." Then she went back into the kitchen, patting my arm as she passed.

I sat alone in the room, rubbing my thumbnail back and forth across the rubbery button of the remote. I didn't know if I should feel sad Mom had gone, or if I should feel relieved. Mostly, I just felt tired. I wished I could rest my mind on something simpler. Something like algebra.

All at once, I couldn't wait to go back to school.

chapter
fifteen

On my first day back to school I wore an outfit that I had once admired on Janice McKenzie—a pale green top and blue jeans with butterfly patches. I wondered if Janice had parted with it of her own free will. Janice's father was the pastor at the Christian Soldiers' Church and Janice had probably been required to purge her closet for the poor, godless Dinsmore/Rickman/Brungard family.

As I walked down the hall to my first class, I could hear my name like an underlying rustle in the air. Dozens of faces turned toward me as I passed. They were talking about *me*, looking at *me*. My breath became shallow from excitement.

My first period was California history and again heads turned toward me as I slid into my seat.

Mr. Reginald nodded. "Good to see you back, Teri."

Doug Stewart came in behind me. He'd obviously gone somewhere sunny on his vacation. His skin was golden brown. He smiled straight at me as he sat down.

"Hey," he said. "You're back. How's it feel?"

I blinked at him in surprise. "Uh—I don't know yet."

"Well, everyone's glad you didn't get hurt in the fire," he said.

I felt my eyebrows push up into my forehead. Jake Bloom leaned over my shoulder from his seat behind me and I could smell bacon on his breath as he said, "Yeah, man, we drove by your house the other day. It was totally roasted. You must have been scared out of your gourd."

Then Corinne Bailey said, "My aunt lives on the other side of Old Man Harrelson. She said she heard screaming the night of the fire. Was it you?"

Doug shot her a look. "Jeez, Corinne, could you be any less subtle?"

"Oh. Sorry," said Corinne, but her eyes were still wide with curiosity.

I shrugged. "Me and Samantha were both screaming at each other. She wanted to go back in the house to call the fire department and I had to stop her."

"Whoa, dude," said Jake. "You probably saved her hide."

They were talking to me like I was a regular person, as if they talked to me this way every day.

The bell rang and everyone turned their heads toward Mr. Reginald. Several times during class Doug looked over and grinned at me. It made little prickles of heat crawl up into my face.

When class was over, Doug got up and stood by the door as if he was waiting for me. I gathered my books and looked uncertainly at him as I started out into the hall. He fell into step beside me. As we walked down the shiny-floored hall with the sound of lockers clanging shut around us, I could feel the startled, happy look on my face.

"I've been thinking about you ever since I heard what happened," Doug said. "What a lousy thing to happen on your birthday."

Air swarmed into my open mouth. "I can't believe you remembered it was my birthday."

"How could I forget when mine is two days after yours?"

"Oh," I said, flustered. "Oh! Then happy birthday. A little late, I guess."

Janice McKenzie appeared at my other side and said, "Hey, that outfit looks really cute on you."

"Uh, thanks." All at once I felt suspicious. Maybe this was all a prank of some sort. I hugged my history book against my chest, afraid to say anything else.

"My dad said to tell you that we prayed for your family at church on Sunday," said Janice. "And he said to invite you and Samantha to services next Sunday."

"Oh. Well." I gave my book a hard squeeze. Janice's father had probably paid for the clothes on my back, so how could I say no without seeming ungrateful? "I don't know. My mom, she doesn't think..." I didn't know how to explain my mother's opinion about going to church on Sunday as being a waste of a perfectly good opportunity to sleep in.

"Hey, I know," said Doug. "If your mom doesn't

want to bring you, me and my dad could pick you up. You could come with us."

Me in the same car with Doug Stewart? I had to say yes. Besides, I still longed to see the inside of a church, the secret land of the Holy Rollers.

"Well, think about it and let me know," Doug said as he increased his pace to get to his next class.

"Wait, I want to go," I said.

Doug turned and walked backward away from me. "Okay, cool. I'll talk to my dad about it tonight." He turned and almost walked straight into Stacey Sorenson. She'd been standing in the middle of the hall waiting for him. They stood with their faces only a few inches apart, talking in low, intimate voices. Stacey's eyes seemed locked somewhere on his chest.

As Janice and I walked by them, she leaned her head close to mine and said, "I'm surprised they're still together after the fight they had."

"Fight?" I squeaked. "What fight?"

"All I know is they totally ignored each other at our Wednesday-night youth group. They must have made up over the break."

I was too impressed to say anything. No one had ever shared gossip with me before.

Janice glanced back at Doug and Stacey. "You know, I saw her last Saturday hanging out in front of Blake's Market with that bunch of Rowdy retards. I bet that's what Doug was mad about."

When I walked into biology class with Janice, all heads turned in unison to look at me, just like before.

Janice loudly said, "What are you geeks staring at?" But they all kept staring anyway. All except Wesley. He sat hunched over his desk, gazing into a book, and he didn't even glance up when I took my seat behind him.

The bell rang and Mr. Scheckel launched into a boring explanation of osmosis. As I copied definitions from the blackboard into my notebook, my eyes kept returning to Wesley's head and the wayward clump of his hair that always pointed in a different direction than the rest. Half the collar on his shirt was rolled under, while the other half was folded out.

Tears lurked behind my eyes. I didn't know why it hurt that Wesley was the only one who hadn't acknowledged what I'd been through. How could I have ever believed that I liked him? Clearly, the intensity of writing the play together had distracted me from my true love for Doug.

I looked down at my notebook and read:

OSMOSIS—the diffusion of a fluid through a semipermeable membrane, resulting in equalization of concentrations on each side.

WESLEY—stupid, geek, dork, hate him

When class was over, Wesley stood and looked at me with a flat expression. "So, I wonder what kind of grade we got on the play."

I looked at him, cold as ice. "I really couldn't care

less." Then I spun and flounced away. Janice was waiting for me at the door.

By fourth period I was getting used to the stares. At least ten people walked right up to me and said they were sorry about what had happened and asked me how I was. They all wanted to know everything about the fire. How did it start? What did I do? How did I feel while it was happening?

I had imagined being popular thousands of times, but my imagination had never come close to what that first day back at school was like. As I walked toward geometry, I actually had a small crowd at my heels listening to me talk about the fire. And after class, when I headed toward the cafeteria for lunch, at least half the people I passed either nodded or said "Hey," even seniors.

When I looked around, everything was the same. The hall still smelled of chalk and dust from the classrooms, oily metal from the lockers and mildew from the ancient heating system. Yet everything was completely different.

I stood at the threshold of the quad, in the doorway facing the mountains. A pine breeze lifted my hair. I closed my eyes and felt all my old, small thoughts blowing through me and away, skittering down the edge of the hall with the dust balls.

I thought, This is the best day of my life.

I went through the line in the cafeteria, at the edge of the steam and sizzle of the kitchen. Every sound echoed against the high ceiling of the eating area. The loud *bang* of someone's book dropping on the floor, a girl yelling, "Give me back my brownie, you butthead!" For the first time, it didn't feel like a wall of sound that excluded me.

As I paid the cashier, Janice came up and pulled me by my elbow to one of the Holy Roller tables. Doug was there, too, but he didn't say much to me. He was too busy glaring at Stacey, who was sitting at a Rowdy table between my sister and Rick Carruthers. As usual Samantha ignored me when I waved.

"I didn't know Stacey and your sister were friends," said Janice as she spread butter on her roll.

I shook my head. "Neither did I."

Samantha's loud laugh carried across the room as Rick stuck straws up his nose and into his ears. Stacey put her lips to one of the straws in his ear and blew into it.

Janice poked Doug on the shoulder. "Hey, I thought you and Stacey were back together."

Doug didn't say anything as he morosely pushed his fork around his chicken noodle casserole.

While Doug tried not to watch Stacey drop peas on Rick's head, I tried not to look at Wesley sitting at his usual table in the middle of the room. When we were working on the play, Wesley and I had eaten lunch together at that table every single day. He didn't seem to be suffering, though. Whatever book he was reading had more of his attention than his food did. He kept a forkful of noodles hovering in front of his face for so long that I wanted to shout, "Just eat it already!"

He was still holding the fork in midair when Randy Mellon sat beside him and leaned to say something in his ear. Wesley listened for a minute, then looked up at me. He stared at me so long and hard that I lost my appetite. I got to my feet, told Janice I'd see her outside, then went to slide my tray through the metal-lined slot to the dishwashing room.

Out of the corner of my eye I saw Wesley hurrying toward me. I pretended I didn't see him and walked toward the square of sunlight at the open double doors. Dust motes swirled out of my way at the door and I was about to step out when Wesley's hand fell on my arm. I turned to meet his red-rimmed eyes.

"I just heard," he said, breathing hard. "About the fire. I didn't know."

I stared at him. "Everyone knows."

"Well, I didn't. And I'm sorry. Really. I can't imagine..." He struggled with his words, his voice tight. "When I think of my house burning down, and losing all my books and everything..."

His eyes filled with tears and for a moment I felt an answering wetness in mine. Then I realized he wasn't ready to cry in sympathy for me; he was just upset at the thought of his own house burning down.

"Yeah. Well," I said. "I'll live." Then I walked away, leaving Wesley squinting into the sunlight.

chapter
sixteen

Although I'd put on a big act for Wesley,
I was really dying to know what grade our play had gotten. But once we got to English class, we found out that
Mrs. Gober had missed her flight home from her Easter
vacation in England. The substitute teacher told us Mrs.
Gober wouldn't be back until Wednesday so we'd have
to wait for our grades.

In the meantime, Janice kept acting like my best
friend, and Doug kept grinning at me during California
history. Part of me knew I was only temporarily interesting to them because of the fire.

"There's a glamour to being a victim," Gramma said
when I told her what had happened at school. But part
of me also wanted to believe that the fire had merely
burned away the shell that had hidden the real, fascinat-
ing me. I liked seeing myself as a phoenix, rising from
the ashes of my old life.

Everything about my life was new. I was fifteen, a
new age. I lived in a new place, I wore all new clothes
and I had a new and dramatic past. Even my face

seemed new to me. When I looked in the mirror, the red spots of pimples didn't leap out at me. I had eyes and a nose and a mouth just like everyone else.

I was beginning to feel almost grateful that the fire had happened. Samantha and I talked about it on Tuesday night as we lay in the dark, waiting to fall asleep. Usually we slept with our backs to each other, but at that moment we lay curled toward each other, stroking the gray cat that lay purring between us.

"I told Brian about how I went in and dragged Andrew out of his room," Samantha said. "He said he's never known a girl as brave as me."

"Corinne Bailey's aunt heard us screaming," I said. "Do you remember us screaming?"

"Kind of. Brian says if I had died in the fire he probably would have killed himself."

"Oh my God. I wish Doug Stewart would say something like that about me."

"I see Doug walking with you. It seems like he likes you."

"What kind of stuff does Stacey say about him?" I asked.

Samantha laughed. "Not a whole lot. She's got the hots for Rick Carruthers now. Doug's all yours."

"No, he's not. He's just being nice to me because of the fire."

"It feels like everything's because of the fire, doesn't it?"

My cheek rubbed against the cool pillow as I nodded. "Yeah."

"Are you sorry it happened?" Samantha asked, her voice a whisper.

I was silent for a long time. I didn't want to say it out loud, but I didn't want to lie, either. "No. Not really."

"Me either."

We didn't know Mom had come home. We didn't know she was in the hall and on the way to the bathroom when she heard us talking. The door banged back against the wall; the cat startled and leapt off the bed.

Mom's silhouette filled the doorway. "So you girls aren't sorry the house burned down. Did I hear you right?" She was using her trembly voice, her betrayed voice.

Samantha and I lay like blocks of cement on the double bed.

"I can't believe this," Mom said. "First Nolan's mother, and now you two! No one cares that my whole life went up in smoke! You care only about yourselves! I can't believe this!"

She banged our door shut. A few seconds later we heard the front door slam. Then we heard her car shooting out of the driveway and the squeal of tires on the street as she roared away.

I groaned out loud. Samantha rose up on her elbow to look at me.

"Don't even bother feeling bad," she said. "I mean it,

Teri. She's the one who always takes off to be with some guy. She's the one who only cares about herself. I'm not about to feel bad."

I struggled against the blankets to sit up. "I *hate* it when you say stuff like that. I don't know why you have to act like Mom doesn't love us. I don't know why you—"

"And I don't know why you defend her all the time!" she yelled. I mean she really yelled. The sound bounced off the walls and crashed into me from all around.

I put a hand to my ear. "Don't do that!"

"Sorry. But Holy Christ..." Samantha flopped over onto her stomach and hugged her pillow. "I just get so tired of the 'poor Mom' crap. You heard what Nolan's mother said. The whole town knows how she's neglected us. Even Andrew knows. You're the only one who hasn't figured it out."

I covered my other ear and began shaking my head. "Don't say that. Don't."

"Why not? It's the truth."

"I don't care!" Now I was the one yelling, raising my voice over the panic rushing up into my throat. "What if she hears you say something like that, then what? What if she doesn't come back anymore? What if she leaves us here with Gramma like she left Andrew with Bill?"

Samantha raised her head and I could feel the intensity of her gaze even through the dark. "Come on, Teri," she whispered. "Think about it. Would that really be so bad?"

She turned back toward the wall. I lay back on my pillow to stare up at the ceiling.

It took me a long time to fall asleep that night.

The next day Mrs. Gober was back and I couldn't help giving Wesley a nervous smile as she passed out the graded plays. Since Wesley's desk was closest to the front, he got the paper first. I craned my neck to see his reaction, but he was gazing down at it with such a vacant expression that I couldn't tell if the grade was good or not.

I got up from my desk. Wesley got up, too, and met me halfway across the back of the room. I snatched the pages out of his hand and the bright red A beamed up at me. We stood there, grinning at each other, while everyone else grumbled and groaned about their grades.

"Seats, please," Mrs. Gober said.

We hurried back to our desks. Mrs. Gober stood at the front of the room, arms crossed over her chest, wearing a stern expression that wasn't very intimidating. She was only about five feet tall, with wispy red hair and a wispy voice to match.

"I was not pleased with the overall results of this assignment," she said. "As a matter of fact, I was downright dismayed."

I slumped down with guilt even though I knew it couldn't have been my work she was criticizing.

"However," said Mrs. Gober, "one drizzly afternoon as I stared into the dirty water of the Thames, I had an epiphany. The best way to learn the mechanics of a good play is to act one out."

More groans met this news, which forced Mrs. Gober to raise her voice. "Of course, Shakespeare was the master, but I think we should probably choose a play that you can relate to a little better. Only one play written in this class earned an A, and I think it's the obvious choice."

My eyes flew to Wesley in alarm. Everyone else was looking around, wondering who the chump was.

"Wesley Wilton and Teresa Dinsmore collaborated on their play, and they did an outstanding job. It's called *The Answer of the Ant,* and I think we'll all learn a lot by performing it here in class."

I shielded my face with my hand, but I could still hear several people snickering. Someone shouted, "Way to go, Prez!"

Mrs. Gober moved to her desk and picked up a stack of paper. "I'm sure you'll all enjoy this little side trip into drama, as we won't be doing any of our regular assignments. I want you to be able to pay close attention to the play."

Several kids applauded while Mrs. Gober walked

across the front of the room, dropping a part of her stack at the front of each row. "I'm passing out copies of the play. I don't want any talking as you read it. At the end of the period you can volunteer for a part you might be interested in playing. However, since Wesley and Teresa wrote the play, I think it would be appropriate if they take the lead roles themselves."

With each sentence Mrs. Gober spoke, my horror deepened. It didn't seem fair that she could make copies of the play without asking permission, then just pass it out in open invitation to ridicule. Then to expect me and Wesley to get up in front of everybody and say the corny lines we'd written...

I waited for Wesley to jump up and object. I waited for him to say that we didn't care to make public jerks of ourselves this week, thank you very much. But Wesley didn't move. Of course not. Wesley Wilton expected to be president of the United States someday; he couldn't let a little classroom play intimidate him. He was probably sitting there thinking what good practice this would be in facing hostile crowds.

If Wesley wasn't going to try to get out of it, then I couldn't. And wasn't this minor compared to escaping a burning building? No one would ever think of me as an intrepid survivor again if I chickened out of my own play.

The sound of ruffling papers filled the room as the pages were passed back along each row. I finally sneaked a look at Wesley and found him grinning happily at Mrs. Gober, his chest puffed out as if he'd written the play all by himself. I wanted to throw a rock at his head.

"Now," said Mrs. Gober, "we don't have a lot of time to spend on this. I don't want it to take any more than a week, so let's shoot for next Tuesday as our performance date. Okay then, let's start reading and we'll discuss it afterward."

Everyone flipped to the first page of the play. I felt my lunch curdling in my stomach. After a minute or so of silence I heard someone at the back of the room mumble, "How stupid."

For the first time that week, I actually missed being invisible.

chapter seventeen

On Thursday Doug Stewart asked me out. For a date. I think I handled it pretty well. I don't think Doug could tell that my insides were lurching up and down like an out-of-control elevator.

"Oooo, a date," I said. "I think I'm too young to date."

"No, you're just right," said Doug.

It was lunchtime on the quad and I was leaning back against an alder just starting to sprout tiny green buds. Doug stood facing me, picking at the bark of the tree beside my arm.

"I don't know," I said. "You probably just want to make Stacey jealous."

"That would be a fringe benefit."

I smiled slowly, closing my eyes against the sun. "So you really want to go out with me?"

"Yeah. Why else would I ask?"

"That's what I'm trying to find out."

"Teri, I want to go out with you."

"Give me one good reason."

Doug grinned as he shook his head. "Man, you're tough."

I reached up to pluck a twig off a branch. "Well, look at it from my point of view. You barely spoke to me before Monday, and now you're asking me out."

"But I was planning to ask you out before me and Stacey...you know."

"Yeah, I totally believe that."

"I'm serious," said Doug. "I always thought you were cute."

My eyes fell to the ground. He was making fun of me. My voice was a whisper as I said, "I'm not...cute."

"Hey, I'm not the only one who thinks so. Jake thinks so, too. And Roger Cahill."

I was shaking my head even before he was finished. "No. If that was true, then why haven't they talked to me before? Or at least said hi to me?"

"Teri," Doug said. "It's hard to talk to someone who walks around looking down and mopey all the time."

I couldn't say a word. It was staggering to think that boys had noticed me before, staggering to think that a male person might have looked at me and not found me ugly. And even more extraordinary was the thought that it might have been my fault that boys had avoided me.

"Come on, Teri," said Doug. He dropped a piece of bark down the back of my blouse. "Do you want to go out with me, yes or no?"

I flapped my blouse away from my back so the bark would fall out. "Yes."

"Tomorrow night?"

"Yes."

"Okay. Was that so hard?"

"Yes."

He laughed and said, "So can I have your phone number?"

Neither of us had any paper, but I did have a pen. He held out his hand and I wrote Gramma's number on his palm. He had big hands, with rough knuckles and square patches of blond hair on his fingers. Doug blew on his palm to make the ink dry faster. Then the bell rang and, after a quick goodbye, I hurried off to English class.

Doug Stewart had said I was cute! He'd asked me out on a date! My most impossible dream was coming true and I felt so light with happiness that my body seemed ready to float away. My cheeks ached from smiling and when we did our first read-through of the play in class, I couldn't keep a laugh out of my voice. Soon half the class was snorting with repressed laughter.

Mrs. Gober pursed her lips and Wesley gave me an aggravated look that only made me laugh harder. Mrs. Gober was struggling to get control of the class when the door opened and Irene Wilton, Wesley's mother, came in and waved at Wesley. Instead of looking embarrassed, Wesley smiled and waved back.

Mrs. Gober held an arm out to Mrs. Wilton. "Class, you all know Mrs. Wilton. She called me last night and offered to help put together some costumes for our play. Of course, the only people who will need costumes are the gypsy, the ballerina and the two doctors."

"And the clown," said Wesley.

"Yes, and the clown. Would those characters please join Mrs. Wilton at the back of the room so that she can take your measurements?"

I watched several kids reluctantly get up to follow Mrs. Wilton. No one was surprised to see her there. She was the PTA president and she always showed up to lend a hand when anything happened at school. She was the one who yelled "Ready, set, go!" at the annual school walkathon, and she was the one who donated the most stuff to bake sales, yard sales and any other fund-raiser that came up.

We continued with the reading, and Wesley spoke his lines in his usual clear and unabashed voice. Mrs. Wilton looked over and beamed at him every few minutes. I felt a pang of envy at their uncomplicated affection for each other. On the few instances my mother was supposed to come to school for an open house or a concert, half the time she didn't show up and the other half she aroused more attention than I could stand.

Thinking about my mother sobered me up and I didn't laugh anymore while reading my lines. I matched my tone to Wesley's, and several times our eyes met as we said the syrupy lines we'd written together.

> STEVE: *I don't know, Marcy. The doctor said my face will always be scarred. Children will always run from me. I don't want that to be part of your life.*
>
> MARCY: *Oh, you fool, you sweet fool. Do you think I care how you look? My heart can't see your face, and my heart decides who I love.*

I said that line and for a minute I couldn't tear my eyes away from Wesley's. I remembered writing those words with him peering over my shoulder, saying, "Yeah, good, that's good." I remembered how we had laughed over some of the ridiculous ideas we came up with. I also remembered how we had talked for hours about serious things, like tragedy and love and the meaning of life.

Someone coughed. I looked down at my pages, flustered. Mrs. Gober had to remind me where we were. I almost blurted out that I didn't want to be in the stupid play, but I didn't. I kept reading, but I didn't look at Wesley again.

That night I waited for Doug to call. I don't think I ever wanted anything like I wanted him to call that night. I sat limp in Gramma's rocking chair, my eyes glued to the phone, unable to do anything but wait.

I barely glanced up when Mom and Nolan came through the front door. From the look on her face, Mom was still angry about what she'd overheard between me and Samantha, so I didn't much mind that she walked through to the kitchen without saying a word.

My eyes homed in on the phone again. I didn't realize that Nolan was still standing by the front door until I heard him say, "Mind if I sit?"

I waved a hand toward the love seat. The floor creaked as he crossed in front of me and sat.

I picked up the phone to make sure there was a dial tone, then quickly hung up.

"Hand me that remote, will you?" he asked. "I want to check the score on the hockey game."

I tossed over the remote and the TV came on. Nolan began flipping through channels that played nothing but static.

"I forgot." Nolan clicked off the TV. "No cable."

In the following silence we could hear Mom and Gramma talking about the fire and the insurance adjuster and the things Mom wanted to add to some kind of list.

I asked Nolan what time it was. He lifted his wrist to check his shiny gold watch and said, "Almost nine o'clock."

My heart shifted down in my chest. It was getting late. Of course, Doug hadn't exactly *said* he'd call, but still, he'd asked for my phone number. Why would he ask me for my number if he didn't plan on calling me?

"You know," Nolan began, "what with the fire, your mom and I never got around to getting you something for your birthday."

I gave him my it's-no-big-deal shrug and wondered if Doug had changed his mind about going out with me. Then I wondered if maybe the whole date thing had been one big joke after all. I imagined getting to school the next morning and seeing Doug and Stacey together in the parking lot, pointing at me, laughing. I imagined walking down the halls with people rolling like barrels across the floor from laughing so hard.

"And I just had a thought," Nolan went on. "How would you like it if we got you cable for a year as a kind of late birthday present?"

I looked up to see big, hulking Nolan chewing on the edge of a fingernail as he waited for my reaction. Then, before I could say anything, he began shaking his head. "Never mind. Bad idea."

"Actually," I said, "cable would be cool."

A smile spread over his face. "Good. That's good. I'll try to call the cable company tomorrow, then."

Mom came out of the kitchen and told Nolan she was ready to go. He winked at me as he got up from the love seat.

Mom stood before me to give me a cool look. "So. You doing okay?"

I gazed up at her. I wanted to tell her everything, about how different things were at school, about how

Doug had asked me out, about how scared I was that he'd changed his mind.

Instead, I said, "Yeah. I guess."

"I've got my pool heater working again," Nolan said as he moved to the front door. "Maybe you guys would like to come down this weekend and do a little swimming."

"Maybe," I said. "Thanks."

Mom gave a fake little smile, then turned and went out the door with Nolan.

I sat next to the phone for another hour before I finally gave up hope that Doug would call. I crawled into bed without brushing my teeth, then lay next to my sleeping sister, taking shallow, aching breaths. I felt sure I'd never be able to forgive Doug. And I'd certainly never be able to trust him again.

The next morning when I slipped behind my desk, my body felt hard and sore from disappointment. Then a hand came from behind me and covered my eyes. I reached up, felt the rough knuckles and in a heavy voice said, "Doug."

He moved his hand. I looked up into his blue eyes and—just like that—it didn't matter that he hadn't called.

"Are we still on for tonight?" he asked.

"Oh, yes," I breathed.

In English, I was so giddy that I kept flubbing my lines during our run-through of the play. After class

Mrs. Gober caught me and Wesley at the door and said she'd hoped to be making better progress by now. She said she couldn't allot any more time to the project, so perhaps Wesley and I should get together over the weekend and rehearse.

I said, "Fine," without too much thought because all my thoughts were busy with Doug.

Wesley said, "How about tomorrow afternoon? My house," he quickly added.

I said, "Okay," and Mrs. Gober said, "Good." Then I went to get ready for gym and I forgot all about going to Wesley's until the next day. And by then, I was a different person.

chapter eighteen

As I waited for Doug to show up at Gramma's, I wished I still had Samantha's purple sweater. Doug had already seen me in all my best donated clothes and I desperately wanted to make an impression that would remain in his mind for all eternity. I had to settle for an olive-green V neck that went with the butterfly-patch jeans.

While Gramma was busy in the kitchen, I sneaked Samantha's makeup bag into the bathroom and brushed on the tiniest bit of eye shadow and mascara. Then I sneaked back into my room so she wouldn't see me while I waited. I had to stand on my bed to see out the window to the street.

I was looking for Doug to come walking up the hill. Instead, a car pulled up and Doug got out of the driver's seat.

With a quick "Bye, Gramma!" I ran out the front door and hurried down the gravel driveway to where Doug stood by the open passenger door. I stopped, out of breath. "But—I mean—your dad lets you drive without a license?"

"Course not." Doug walked around and slid into the seat beside me. "I just got my license last week. Want to see it?"

"You're sixteen?"

He leaned forward to dig his wallet out of his back pocket. "Yeah. My birthday's two days after yours, remember?"

"But—you're a freshman."

"Yeah, well, I kinda got held back in sixth grade." He handed me his license.

I looked at him, bemused. Perfect Doug Stewart had flunked a grade? Then I looked down at his license and went into shock. He looked like somebody else with his eyes half closed and a strand of hair sticking up like a bug antenna.

"Wow," was all I could think of to say as I handed it back.

Doug started the car and pulled onto the street. "I thought we'd go by the theater and see what movie's playing, okay?"

I nodded and wished my smile felt more natural.

It took only two minutes to get to the theater; one left turn and we were there. The sidewalk in front of the theater was overrun with kids. The movie was an animated Disney fairy tale that Mom had been promising to take me and Andrew to see since Christmas. I would have liked to see it, but Doug just sighed and continued down Main.

"Well," he said. "There's always bowling. Do you bowl?"

"No," I said dully, remembering the times I'd overheard Doug telling Jake how he bowled game after game with Stacey.

Doug sighed again. "I guess we could walk down Main and get a shake at Maggie Moo's," he said.

That sounded fine to me, but Doug's voice was flat with disappointment. He parked, and we got out and started walking. Doug reached for my hand but I didn't realize what he was doing. He dropped his hand at the same moment I offered mine. I quickly raised my hand to my head as if I'd only meant to scratch an itch.

We passed the Shear Magic Hair Salon, Gramma's main competitor; the Bank of America; the steak house; the Timberville Book Stop. I couldn't stop looking at our blurred reflections in the store windows. Maybe I'd seen Doug with Stacey Sorenson too many times, but he just didn't look right with me.

We'd started by the Wagon Wheel Saloon when I noticed Bill Rickman's truck parked out front. I stopped still. If Bill was in the saloon, then who was watching Andrew? It would be just like Bill to leave Andrew alone while he went out drinking.

I grabbed Doug's arm. "Would you mind taking me

to see my brother first? Just for a minute? I haven't seen him in a while."

"Uh, sure, I guess so."

We went back to the car and I gave him directions to Bill's house, which was only a couple of miles outside town. The dirt driveway was empty when Doug pulled in. I was out and running to the front door before Doug had even turned the car off.

I banged on the door and a few seconds later Andrew opened it. He stood, staring at me, his face smeared with something brown and sticky. I pulled him close in a hug, ready to carry him out to Doug's car and take him home to Gramma's.

Then the door opened a little wider and a plump blond woman wearing a bathrobe gave me a sour look.

I straightened in surprise. "Oh!"

"You must be one of the sisters," said the woman. "I'm Shirley."

Andrew made a face. "Dad's girlfriend."

Shirley hooked a hand over Andrew's shoulder and pulled him back out of the way. "Come in, if you want."

I looked uncertainly back at Doug, who was just stepping up onto the tiny porch. He seemed to expect to follow me in so I went through the door after Andrew.

The living room was dim and cluttered. Two chairs were crammed up against the wall, while the couch was adrift in the middle of the room. Shirley gathered a bunch of newspapers off the floor. "The house is a mess.

I just woke up. I work the graveyard shift at the mill. Go ahead, have a seat if you want."

Doug gave me a tight smile. I knew he didn't want to be there, but then, neither did I. All I'd really wanted was to make sure Andrew was okay, but Andrew didn't seem too interested in me. He'd already dropped back down in front of the television to finish the Nintendo game we'd interrupted.

"Well," said Shirley. "I have to take a shower. Andrew, if the phone rings, answer it."

Shirley disappeared down a dark hall. I stared after her. I couldn't believe Bill had called my mother a whore for kissing Nolan when he was *living* with another woman.

I turned back to look at my brother. "So, how've you been, Andrew?"

He didn't bother to turn away from the TV as he said, "Pretty good."

The TV emitted a series of beeps and the words GAME OVER appeared on the screen. Andrew hit the ground with his fist and yelled, "Shit!"

Doug raised his eyebrows at me. I nodded and started toward the door. "Andrew, we're gonna go, okay? I just wanted to see if you were all right."

Andrew didn't say anything. He was already starting a new game.

As I followed Doug out, I wondered if Andrew would even remember I'd been there. I didn't blame him too much. He'd given me about as much attention as I used to give him when I was trying to read a book and he was begging me to play Candy Land. Now, with each step I took away from Bill's house, I felt worse. If I'd been a better sister, I would have played with him more. If I'd been a better sister, he'd have wanted to go home with me.

Back in the car, Doug turned the key in the ignition. "Well, where to now?"

I didn't answer. I had no idea where to go, and right then I didn't much care.

Then Doug said, "Can we go see your old house?"

I stared at him. In the quiet I could hear faint static coming from the radio.

"Um, sure, I guess," I finally said. "If you want to."

He pulled out onto the street. "Are you sure?"

I shrugged one shoulder, pretending it wasn't weird that he wanted to go visit my burned, empty house. "Yeah. I mean, if you really want to."

He must have really wanted to, because he stepped on the gas and went way past the speed limit the two miles back to town.

When we stopped in front of the blackened house, I tried to look at it as Doug was seeing it. Was he imagining it the way it had been the night of the fire, with flames writhing against the sky? Was he imagining me running out of the smoke in my nightgown?

It was sunset as we walked through the front door.

The light at the windows was weak and orange and left most of the living room in shadows. The whole place reeked of soot and mildew from the water that still hadn't dried in places.

Doug's eyes glittered as he looked around. I stood in the middle of the room, trying to look tragic but brave.

Doug disappeared into the hall and I heard him say, "Oh, man," several times. He came back into the living room, shaking his head. "Oh, man. It's a miracle you all got out."

I nodded. I didn't want to disillusion him by saying the smoke alarm had probably warned us in plenty of time.

"What's in there?" he asked, pointing.

"The kitchen. It didn't catch."

"Then we could hang out in there for a while, couldn't we?" He walked into the kitchen and I followed.

I pushed the smoke-darkened curtains away from the windows to let in the last of the light. While Doug stared out the window over the sink at the silhouette of the mountains, I got a dish towel out of a drawer and wiped the layer of soot and ash from the kitchen chairs. I offered him a seat as if it was a normal chair in a normal house.

"I'm sorry I asked you to go Bill's house," I said. "I guess I'm a pretty lousy date."

"No, you're not," he said, but I knew he was just

being polite. Then he leaned back in his chair and said, "Too bad I don't have any pot. But I know who has some if you want to get high."

I went into shock for the second time that night. Doug Stewart smoked marijuana?

He was waiting for me to say something, so I said, "Who?"

"Janice McKenzie."

I tried to nod as if it was no big surprise to me that the minister's daughter smoked pot, too.

"Do you want some?" he asked.

"Umm, not really." But then I was afraid he would think me totally uncool so I said, "There might be some beer around, though."

I got up and opened the refrigerator door. A horrible, rotting mold odor rolled out and made me gasp. There was no beer, but just before I slammed the door shut, I spotted several bottles of wine inside the door rack and yanked one out.

I held up the bottle. "It's never been opened. It's probably okay."

"Score!" Doug shouted, which made me feel pleased and annoyed at the same time. Was drinking the only way he could get enthusiastic about this date? But then, I was the one who had grabbed the bottle in the first place. Maybe I was the one looking for some enthusiasm.

Doug took the bottle and squinted at the label.

"White zinfandel. Sounds good to me." I got a corkscrew out of the utensil drawer and handed it to him.

The sky outside was purple-pink now, and inside the darkening kitchen Doug's face was losing all color, like the picture on a black-and-white television. He grunted as he struggled with the corkscrew, then finally held up the cork in triumph. He took a long swallow, then handed the bottle to me.

I took a tiny sip and was surprised at the wine's sweet taste. I took a bigger gulp, then another. It went down nice and easy and less than a minute seemed to have passed before a warm heaviness began creeping through my arms and legs.

We passed the bottle back and forth and, in an effort to keep some kind of conversation going, we asked each other, "So what do you want to do after you graduate?" But neither of us knew what we wanted to be yet.

"I don't know," Doug said as he went to the refrigerator and took out a second bottle of wine. "It just seems like it's so far away."

He poised the corkscrew over the bottle and started twisting. "Things change every day and any effort you make planning things is wasted energy."

I nodded, but as I took the second bottle from him and tilted it up for a drink, I couldn't help thinking of Wesley and his plan to be president. He'd even narrowed down the year of his election. And Wesley would never have given me a polite denial when I said I was a lousy date. He would have said something like "Yeah, well, next time I'll plan the agenda."

Why was I thinking of Wesley? I was probably getting drunk. My thoughts seemed to be moving through my head extra slow and sticky, like syrup. Even my tongue felt slow as I said to Doug, "I know what you mean. You can't count on anything. Like I thought I'd live in this house until I—"

In the middle of my sentence, I belched. I hadn't felt it coming. I covered my mouth with my hand but Doug was already laughing. Then he was quiet a moment and into the silence came a resounding burp from his mouth. He laughed even harder and probably thought I'd join in. But I was too busy crying.

I hadn't felt it coming any more than I had the belch. All of a sudden, hot tears were sliding down my nose, and my shoulders were bouncing with sobs.

Doug groped for me through the dark and his voice broke against my ear. "Hey, I'm sorry. I shouldn't have laughed. But it's no big deal."

I didn't want him to think I was falling apart because of a stupid burp so I said, "No, it's not that. It's the fire."

Doug kept patting my shoulder until I pushed his hand away. I wished I could just flop onto the floor and cry until I felt better, but I couldn't do that with Doug there, so I stood and said, "I want to go home."

He got up. "Yeah, sure, whatever you want." Then

he tripped over my foot in the dark. That made him start laughing all over again. He laughed so hard he snorted and bumped into the chair, the counter, the wall. I walked around him, out of the kitchen and out the front door.

Doug took a while to calm down and get in the car. On the way home I kept wiping at my runny nose. "I'm sorry. I think it was the wine. I drank too much."

"No, look, it's okay. Don't apologize. I'm the one who asked you to go there."

But when he stopped the car in front of Gramma's trailer, I said it again. "I'm sorry."

"Teri," he said, and he turned to look at me. We were parked right under a streetlight and I hated that he could see my puffy eyes and wet nose. He leaned toward me as if he was going to kiss me. I automatically leaned back and my elbow must have pressed on the door handle, because the door cracked open behind me and I had to grab the dashboard to keep from falling out. Then Doug turned back to the steering wheel and my chance to be kissed was gone before I'd decided if I even wanted it or not.

I pushed the door all the way open. "Um, thanks for asking me out." I said it in a way that let him know I didn't expect him to ask again. But no one can say Doug Stewart doesn't have good manners.

"Thanks for coming," he said. "So I'll see you Sunday, then. You're still coming to church, right?"

"If you still want me to."

"Sure. Why not?"

I nodded. "Well . . ." I stood up beside the door. "Goodbye, I guess."

He gave me a little wave and I shut the door.

The car pulled away. I watched until the red taillights turned the corner and disappeared.

As soon as Doug drove away, I felt the dull throbbing of a headache in my temples. And my stomach hurt. I wanted my bed.

I stumbled up the gravel driveway, pushed through the front door and was halfway across the living room before I noticed Gramma and Samantha sitting there, both gazing fixedly at the TV. But the TV wasn't turned on.

I looked from one to the other. Gramma's lips were white and Samantha's cheeks glowed with bright red patches of emotion.

"What's going on?" I asked.

Gramma turned over the dish towel draped across her lap. "Will you tell her or shall I?"

Samantha raised her chin. "Brian's moving to Los Angeles next week. I'm going with him."

Gramma began folding the towel into a tiny square. "With only two months to go until graduation, she's going to drop out because of a boy."

"I have to!" Samantha cried. "I can't live without Brian. I'd die!"

"Rubbish!" Gramma clenched the towel in her fist and stood. "Do you know how many times your mother has said those very same words to me? Do you not see the irony in the fact that *you*—the one who judges her most harshly—are repeating her life in exact detail?"

Samantha's face darkened. "It's not even close to the same thing."

"You don't think so? Your mother dropped out of school to elope with your father two and a half months before she would have graduated."

"Really?" I said with a laugh of surprise.

Gramma turned to look sternly at me. I slapped my hand over my mouth, afraid she'd know I'd been drinking.

"If you girls, both of you," she said, sweeping the dish towel toward me, "if you start depending on a man to give your life meaning, then it turns into a habit. And it's a hard habit to break. Just ask your mother."

We both watched her go into her bedroom and shut the door behind her. I turned to Samantha, tried to focus. "You're really going to drop out of school?"

"Oh, what do you care?" she said as she headed for the door. "I'm going to see Brian and tell him about all the love and support I get from my family."

I stood in the quiet living room. The floor seemed to be tilting. I was still high on the wine and knew trying to think about anything important would be useless. I wobbled into my room, fell onto the bed and held on until it spun me to sleep.

I woke in the middle of the night with a horrible headache and a desperate need for a drink of water. I stumbled down the dark hall and through the living room toward the kitchen. I stopped short at the sight of Gramma sitting in her bathrobe in a dim pool of light from the table lamp. She was holding the framed photo of my mother as a teenager that usually sat beside the lamp. She was staring down at it as if she'd never seen it before.

I squinted at her. "Gramma? You okay?"

She didn't look up and I thought maybe she hadn't heard me. "Gramma?" I said again.

She looked up at me, and for once her face wasn't blank. Her eyes were full of tears that seeped into the creases of her skin.

"Your mother was thirteen when her father died. Only thirteen. She was wild with grief and she needed me to comfort her. But I didn't have it in me. I could barely get myself out of bed, let alone help her." Gramma ran her sleeve around the gold edge of the picture's frame. "I suppose in many ways she's still waiting to be comforted."

She set the photo back in its place on the table. "You can love your children more than anything. That doesn't mean you won't hurt them. That doesn't mean you can always be the mother they need you to be."

I took a step toward her. "Gramma," I began.

She stood and waved me away. "It's late," she said

briskly. "I called your mother. She'll be here first thing in the morning. Go on and get some sleep now."

She gave me a quick pat on the shoulder as she passed, then disappeared into her bedroom and shut the door.

I wandered back toward my own bed, my hand to my still-pounding head. The next thing I knew, I was under the sheets and sliding back down toward the edge of sleep. I wondered before falling away if I'd really seen Gramma cry, or if the whole thing had been a dream.

chapter
nineteen

When I woke late the next morning, my brain felt swollen, too big for my skull. As I walked to the bathroom, my legs shook. When I looked in the mirror, even my reflection seemed to shiver against the glass. My first hangover. And absolutely my last.

I took three Advil and went to lie down again. Then I heard my mother's voice weaving between Gramma's and Samantha's beyond my door. I yanked on my clothes and hurried into the kitchen.

Samantha was sitting at the table, staring sullenly at the salt shaker. She was gritting her teeth so hard that her jaw was thrust out to one side.

Mom and Gramma stood by the sink. Gramma held on to the counter while Mom gripped her own side, as if she was winded. Mom's hair was pulled back into a haphazard ponytail; she wore no makeup. She looked like a stranger standing in Gramma's kitchen.

"Your children think you've abandoned them," Gramma was saying.

"No!" Mom's eyes blazed. "They've abandoned *me*. I tried to get Andrew but he said he wanted to stay with his father. 'Dad has Nintendo,' he said. And the girls, they're happier without me. I heard them say it."

"Mom." I stepped into the middle of the room. "That's not true."

Mom swung her head around to me. "I heard you! You're not sorry about the fire, you're not sorry I lost everything."

A familiar panic gripped me. I had to say something quick, before she disappeared behind a slammed door. "I am sorry," I said in a shaking voice. "I am."

Mom looked at Samantha, sitting hard and still, then back at me. "Does that mean you'll come down to Redding and live with Nolan and me?"

My stomach clenched tight. Now that school was getting bearable, she wanted me to leave? I didn't want to go. But if I said no, she would go without me. She would leave me behind and I would lose my mother.

"Teri?" Mom prodded, her voice cracking.

I couldn't answer her. I couldn't make such a terrible choice.

But my silence was answer enough for Mom. She turned fiercely on Gramma. "You see? They don't care about me. Why should I care what Samantha does? She can go to Timbuktu if she wants. I don't care!"

Mom turned for the back door. I started after her

with a cry of "Mommy!" But Samantha flew by me and flung herself in front of Mom, blocking the door with her body.

"Oh, no you don't," Samantha growled. "This isn't even about you. This is about *me*, and for once you're going to stick around and listen to how *I* feel."

Mom stepped back, her face shutting down, her hands coming up as if to ward off a blow. I was already moving toward her when Samantha stepped between us.

"Stop it!" she yelled in my face. "Stop protecting her all the time! And you, too!" She pointed a finger at Gramma. "You all act as if she's so fragile, as if her feelings are the only ones that matter. Well, guess what? My feelings are important, too!"

Samantha spun around to Mom, her face scrunched up with tears she was too stubborn to shed. "Do you hear me, Mom? I'm important, too!"

Mom was nodding, her mouth opening as if she wanted to say something, but Samantha didn't wait for her to get it out.

"But you know what else?" she demanded. "I didn't know I was important. Brian is the one who showed me that. Brian is the only person in my whole stupid life who's ever acted like *I'm* the center of the universe. And I'm not giving that up. Even if I *do* have to move to Timbuktu, I'm not giving him up!"

Samantha turned and jerked the door open, then

plunged out into the gray morning. We heard her running across the gravel as the door drifted further open, then slowly began to drift back.

Mom put her hands to her cheeks, breathing hard. Her eyes moved to mine in a look of shock. Then her hands drifted down and she patted herself, as if surprised she was still in one piece. I reached out to pull the door shut.

Mom's eyes slid over to Gramma. "I suppose you're going to tell me I deserved all that."

Gramma moved to the table and lowered herself wearily into a chair. "I'm not the one who decides who deserves what."

Mom's shoulders caved in. She crossed over to the table and sat in the chair opposite Gramma. She hooked her finger in the handle of her coffee mug, but she didn't drink. I shuffled over to sit down between them.

Mom lifted watery eyes to me. "You know how much you matter to me, don't you, Teri? You know you're more important to me than my own life, don't you?"

I gazed down at the thin yellow lines of the vinyl tablecloth. I heard Samantha's voice ringing in my head: *Stop protecting her.* I looked up at Mom, a flood of emotion rising inside me. But before I could form it into words, Gramma said, "Of course she knows."

I dropped my eyes back to the table. A voice in my head asked, *Do I really know that? Do I?*

Mom reached out to squeeze my arm. "And you know that I want you to come live with me in Redding, right? You don't think I'm abandoning you, do you?"

I didn't look up as I said, "No."

"Then you understand? You understand why I have to go? You understand why, just once in my life, I need to be able to start fresh?"

I nodded. I did understand that, more than she knew.

"Thank you," she whispered. Then she put her arms around me and squeezed. My hands came up and I clung to her for a long moment. Then I made myself let go.

"I have to get going," she said with a loud sniff. "I have an appointment with the fire investigator."

Gramma wanted to know if she'd get a copy of the report, and Mom said of course she would. Then Mom said, "I'll call you," and pressed a kiss to the side of my head.

I didn't look up; I just sat and listened as the back door opened, then clunked shut behind her. A moment later, Gramma's chair scraped against the floor and I heard her walk into the living room.

I sat alone, listening to the ticking of the stove clock. All this, I thought, all this is because of the fire. I was sure that if our house had still been standing, none of this would have been happening. We'd all be safely tucked in our rooms instead of flying apart. And I felt now exactly as I'd felt the night I watched our house burn down—frozen and helpless to do anything to stop it.

I pulled myself out of the chair, went to my room and shut the door. Then I did the only thing I could think of: I pressed my face into my pillow and screamed.

As I walked to Wesley's house that afternoon, my head still hurt and I still felt a scream of frustration building up in my throat. I couldn't believe Samantha was really going to leave. It seemed indescribably dumb. Then I remembered how I'd felt just a few days earlier, waiting for Doug to call me, and how I'd have gladly traded everything I owned if only it would have made the phone ring.

I winced at the thought of Doug. Tomorrow I would see him again, and how would he act when he saw me? Did he regret asking me out? Was there any chance that he'd ask me out again?

Maybe I could do something to repair the damage. Maybe I could ask him to pretend that the night before had never happened. We could call a redo, rewind the tape to the part where I was standing on my bed watching through the window as he drove up in his dad's car to pick me up. First Date: Take Two.

But was that what I really wanted?

The lawn of Wesley's house was covered with wooden ducks and flowers and a sign painted to look like the backside of a woman bending over. Mrs. Wilton opened the front door with a cheerful "Hello, Teresa! So nice to see you. Please come in."

I had to smile in return. If Mrs. Wilton was on a sinking ship, she'd still be smiling and waving to everyone as they jumped into shark-infested waters.

As I stepped into the living room, I stared at the profusion of handmade crafts all over the walls and shelves. Even the furniture was layered with afghans Mrs. Wilton had made herself. Mrs. Wilton stuck her head into a hallway and yelled, "Wesley, honey, your friend is here!" Then she introduced me to her husband, Roy, who sat in a recliner, chewing on an unlit pipe and reading a magazine about computers. He lifted his pipe in greeting but didn't say anything. He looked a lot like Wesley, only with a thicker waist, a thicker nose and thinner hair.

Wesley came in, blinking like someone who'd just come out of the dark. Mrs. Wilton slid an arm around his shoulders and squeezed. "Roy and I are just so proud of the two of you, having your class produce your play. It's just so exciting! Oh, Teresa, would you like to see the costumes? I'm nearly finished."

"Later, Ma, okay?" said Wesley. "We've got a lot of work to do." I thanked Mrs. Wilton, then followed Wesley down a picture-lined hall.

Inside Wesley's room one wall was a mass of shelves crammed with books. The opposite wall was covered with posters, but not posters of musicians like most kids would have. They were posters of presidents or would-be presidents like Thomas Jefferson and Abraham Lincoln and Robert Kennedy.

"Nice room," I said, sitting on the patchwork quilt draped across the foot of the bed.

"Thanks." Wesley sat at a child-sized desk and rested his arms along the chair back. "Sorry about my mom."

"It's okay. She's nice. So's your dad."

"Yeah. They're nice people."

"You seem to get along with them pretty well."

"Not as well as I used to," said Wesley. "They're upset because I plan to be a Democrat."

I started to laugh, but my heart wasn't in it. Wesley dropped his chin onto his arms to study me.

"You look depressed," he said.

I shrugged. "It's just my family." Then it all came rushing out. "My brother is living with my jerk of a stepfather, and my mother is moving to Redding to live with her boyfriend, and my sister is about to go to Los Angeles with Brian Webber, and I don't want any of them to go. I want things to be the way they were before the fire, but not really, because before the fire I was miserable and—oh, I don't know!"

I wiped at my tears before they had a chance to fall. Wesley just sat there, staring at me, and suddenly I was mad at him, too.

"And you!" I yelled. "Before the fire no one talked to

me but you. Now everyone talks to me *except* for you, and I don't even know why."

Wesley jerked upright. "Hey, it wasn't me who changed, it was you. I thought we were friends, then all of a sudden you start acting like a girl."

"What a stupid thing to say. How else am I supposed to act?"

"I don't know!" he yelled.

"What have you got against girls, anyway?"

"Nothing!"

"Then what's your problem?"

"I don't have one!"

We stared hotly at each other across the room. Then came a quick knock and Mrs. Wilton swung the door open. "Milk and cookies!" She stepped inside with a tray bearing a plate of oatmeal cookies and two glasses of milk.

"It sounds like a very passionate play," Mrs. Wilton said as she set the tray down on the desk beside Wesley. "Your father and I can hear you all the way into the living room."

I rolled my lips in to keep from laughing.

"Enjoy!" sang Mrs. Wilton as she walked out and closed the door behind her.

Wesley tossed me a cookie, then bit into his own. "So why were you miserable before the fire?"

I stared down at my cookie. I couldn't tell him it was

because I'd begun to like him so much and he hadn't liked me back. All that was ancient history, and besides, I still had a possible relationship brewing with Doug. But sitting there with Wesley, I could hardly remember what Doug looked like. Suddenly all I wanted was for Wesley to throw his cookie aside and grab me and kiss me for about an hour.

Wait a minute, I thought. How could I be madly in love with Doug one day and want Wesley to kiss me the next? No wonder Wesley was wary of girls.

"Never mind," said Wesley. "Let's just practice our lines, okay?"

I sighed and lay back on the bed. "Okay. You start."

I nibbled on the cookie between my lines, reciting them from memory without a single mistake. About halfway through, Wesley stopped me and said, "Why are we practicing? You know your lines."

"I should," I said. "I wrote them."

"Then why did you keep messing up in class yesterday?"

"I don't know. Yesterday I was a different person."

"What's that supposed to mean?"

"Nothing. Can I have another cookie?"

Wesley threw another cookie and it landed on my stomach. I took a big bite out of it and listened to the sound of my own chewing in my ears. When I'd eaten the whole thing, I got up to get my glass of milk. Wesley sat there, watching me drink. I swept my tongue over my upper lip so I wouldn't have a milk mustache. Wesley abruptly dropped his eyes.

"I've been thinking," he said.

"About what?"

"That we should change the end of the play."

"Why?"

Wesley put a half-eaten cookie back on the plate and carefully wiped the crumbs from his hands. "Because. We have Marcy telling Steve she loves him no matter what he looks like, but we don't give any action to prove it."

"Like what?"

Wesley met my eyes, then looked away. "Well, we have Steve kissing the hem of Marcy's skirt before he gets mangled. Maybe Marcy should kiss Steve after he's mangled. You know, to prove her love. I think it would be a powerful action, considering..."

Amazingly, my voice was steady as I said, "Yeah. You've got a point."

He looked at me again and my heart stumbled at the contact of his brown eyes. This time I looked away first.

"What about Mrs. Gober?" I asked. "Will she let us change it?"

"Why not? Writers always make changes in mid-production."

I stared intently down at the brown shag of the carpet. This could only mean one thing. Wesley wanted to kiss me. Maybe even as much as I wanted to kiss him. I felt heat crawl up into my face and I had to take several deep breaths before I could talk.

"Okay," I croaked. "I'll do it if you will."

"Well, I think it's essential to the integrity of our theme."

I nodded earnestly. "Oh, yes, I agree. I don't know why we didn't write it that way in the first place."

"So then, we'll do it. Right after Marcy says, 'My heart decides who I love.'"

"Okay." I held out my hand and we shook on it. "But no backing out at the last minute."

Wesley gave me an annoyed look. "I wouldn't do that."

I laughed and grabbed another cookie. My birthday wish was going to come true after all.

Later, Mrs. Wilton invited me to stay for dinner. We ate pot roast and homemade rolls, and Mr. Wilton told funny stories about running into bears while working in the woods. Then, out of nowhere, he asked me how my family was holding up since the fire.

My smile dissolved. "Oh. Well," I said over the lump of emotion in my throat. "Okay, I guess."

Mr. Wilton leaned back in his chair to cross his arms over his rounded middle. "I find fire to be a very interesting phenomenon. Did you know that if it wasn't for the periodic sweep of fire, our forests wouldn't be able to thrive?"

I resisted the urge to say "So what?" and shook my head.

"It's true," he said. "Fire is the means by which the forest is continually regenerated. There's nothing like a good wildfire to consume the dead vegetation that accumulates on the forest floor and clear the way for new growth."

"Oh," I said, although I didn't really see what forest fires had to do with someone's house burning down.

Mr. Wilton leaned forward. "In fact, some species depend almost entirely on fire to spread their seeds. The jack pine, for instance, produces a resin-filled cone that—"

"Dad," Wesley interrupted. "I was hoping to show Teri your garden before it got too dark."

"Oh, sure, sure," Mr. Wilton said with a pleased smile. "Great idea, go right ahead."

I gave Wesley a look of gratitude, then told Mrs. Wilton how good dinner had been and thanked them both about three times before I got up to follow Wesley out the sliding back door.

He was waiting for me on the deck, his hands stuffed into his pockets. "We don't really have to look at the garden. It's just my dad; once he gets going about something, it's hard to get him to stop."

"Kinda like you," I said, but his feet were already thumping down the wooden steps that led to the back gate, so he didn't hear me.

"Come on," he said over his shoulder, "I'll walk you to the corner."

We walked together to the end of his block, then stood there talking while the light seeped out of the sky and moths orbited the streetlight over our heads. I told him about how I used to think the ridge of mountains to the west held back the ocean. He told me about how he used to have a crush on Mrs. Gober.

I gave him a startled laugh. "You're kidding."

"Well, she's a good person."

"Sounds like your crush is still alive and well."

"It's not," he said.

"How do you know?"

He gave me a long look. "Because."

We stayed out there talking until my teeth chattered from the cold, and still I didn't want to say good night. Mr. Wilton finally came out and asked me if I wanted a ride home, and I was too cold to refuse. Wesley came along, riding in back, and I sat in the front in a cloud of smoke from Mr. Wilton's pipe. I felt Wesley's eyes on me the whole way.

chapter

twenty

Doug knocked at Gramma's front door on Sunday morning at 9:45, exactly the time he said he'd be there. He smiled at me as I stepped from the trailer into the morning sun.

"You look nice," he said, ever the gentleman.

"Thank you. You look nice, too." And he did. His hair was still wet and smooth, and he wore a long-sleeved blue shirt that made his eyes look the same color as the sky.

He opened the back door of his car for me, then slid into the front seat next to his father. "Dad," he said, "this is Teresa Dinsmore. Teri, this is my father, Peter Stewart."

Mr. Stewart's blue eyes met mine in the rearview mirror. "Glad to meet you, Teri. And I'm especially glad you're coming to church with us today."

I said I was glad to be there, and for the rest of the three-minute drive Mr. Stewart told me how sad he had been to hear about the fire and how much he prayed for our family. Doug kept looking back at me as if he expected me to burst into tears at any minute.

We pulled into a gravel parking lot and before I was even all the way out of the car, several people approached me with face-splitting smiles. They squeezed my shoulder and told me how happy they were to see me. I didn't understand why my presence should cause such an outbreak of joy, but apparently it did.

Janice came up to me, too, wearing a pale yellow dress. She said she was glad I could make it and did I want to sit with her? I glanced at Doug. He took my hand and said, "No, she's with us," which I thought was nice.

The church was a square white building, not very big. Once inside, I was surprised to find an unadorned white room with about ten pews on each side and a simple lectern in front. All the churches I'd seen on TV had stained-glass windows and statues and altars.

The pastor, at least, didn't disappoint. He was Pastor McKenzie, Janice's father, and once the sermon began, he was just like the preachers I'd seen on TV. He raised his arms toward heaven and called out, "Almighty God, I pray that you open the hearts of all those assembled! Open their hearts to the truth, O Lord!"

My heart did feel open. And I wanted to know the truth about God; I'd wanted to know for a long time. I sat forward, ready.

Unfortunately, Pastor McKenzie didn't talk about God that day. He talked instead about the devil. And hell. He talked about hell for almost an hour. It got

pretty bizarre at times, the way he described people being tortured in hell with their skin peeling off from the
heat and their voices ruined from screaming. Sometimes
it was hard not to laugh. It reminded me of listening to
Mrs. Gober read a story by Edgar Allan Poe and seemed
about as relevant to my life.

After the sermon, everyone got up to sing about the
blood of the lamb, whatever that meant. I noticed that
even though Doug moved his lips, he didn't actually
sing along. Then Pastor McKenzie said another prayer,
asking that everyone be granted a safe journey home,
and that was it. Everyone started talking and walking at
a snail's pace to the doors.

I hid my disappointment as I wandered back out into
the sun with Doug. He stood with me on the damp lawn
of the church and said, "So. Nice day, huh?"

I nodded, taking in the snow-topped peaks filling up
the horizon.

"Pretty radical sermon," he said.

I nodded again.

"Well, some of it you can't take too seriously."

"I guess not."

I felt Doug stiffen beside me a moment before I saw
Stacey Sorenson coming up the walk. She wore shorts
even though it was barely sixty degrees. I could see the
goose bumps on her perfect legs.

She didn't even glance at me; she just stared straight
at Doug and said, "Can I talk to you?" She turned and

walked away without waiting for an answer and, of course, Doug followed.

The funny thing was, I didn't care. I really didn't. Sure, Doug was nice, and it would have been easy to keep thinking I was in love with him. And it would have been just as easy to hate myself because he didn't like me as much as he liked Stacey. But why should I put myself through that? I hardly knew Doug.

But I knew Wesley Wilton. I had written a play with him and learned what was important to him. I knew he believed in books and learning and working hard to be somebody. I knew he was honest to a fault. And I knew that even if he had a lousy voice, Wesley would still sing the hymns at church loud enough for everyone to hear.

I wondered what church the Wilton family went to. I still wanted to learn more about God. Maybe in Wesley's church they actually talked about God on Sundays. I'd ask him next time I saw him. I'd ask him what he thought about God and religion and no doubt he'd start pontificating in his superior way until I'd have to tell him to shut up.

I smiled to myself. Then I went to find Mr. Stewart to tell him I'd decided to walk home.

On Monday I was so upset about Samantha leaving that I didn't go to school. Instead, I followed her around the trailer, tossing insults at her.

"You're a liar," I said. "A liar and a coward."

"What is your problem?" She demanded as she snapped her suitcase shut.

"You said you were going to be a graphic artist. You said you weren't going to end up like Mom."

She stared down at her suitcase. "I'm still going to be a graphic artist."

"No, you're not. You think art schools take high school dropouts?"

She tried for her usual sarcastic smile. "Is this some lame attempt at reverse psychology? You think I'll stay just to prove you wrong?"

"I don't care why you stay. Just stay, okay?"

"Holy Christ!" she shouted, throwing her arms in the air as she advanced on me. "If you don't stop it I'm gonna knock you flat. Don't you think this is hard enough for me?"

"Then don't go!" I shouted back.

She shoved me into the hall and slammed the bedroom door in my face.

When Brian pulled up in his Camaro outside and honked, Samantha shuffled out of the bedroom, her head down so low that her hair hung in her face.

Gramma handed Samantha a paper sack full of canned food. "At least I know you won't go hungry." She hugged Samantha. "You're allowed to change your mind, you know."

Samantha was crying when she pulled away from Gramma; then she stumbled into me and kissed me hard, right on the mouth. My face was wet with her tears as she ran out the front door.

Gramma slowly lowered herself into her rocking chair and set her chin in her hand, her face betraying nothing.

I threw myself on the couch and cried extravagantly. I cried because I wouldn't step on Andrew's Matchbox cars anymore, and because my mother wouldn't yell at me to do the dishes, and I wouldn't fight with Samantha over the bathroom ever again. I'd believed I hadn't lost anything in the fire, but I had. I'd lost my family.

Gramma finished drinking the coffee out of her World's Greatest Grandma mug. "Well. I suppose I'd better get to work."

I heard water running in the bathroom as she brushed her teeth. She came out rubbing lotion into her hands. Just as she was dropping her keys into her purse, we heard the unmistakable rumble of Brian's Camaro in front of the trailer.

Gramma and I met at the front window and watched as Samantha got out of the car and carried her suitcase up the driveway. Gramma calmly pulled the front door open.

Samantha stood in the doorway, her hair bright with the sun. "You said I could change my mind."

Gramma put her fingers to her mouth and nodded.

Samantha turned to watch Brian drive away. "I love him. I really love him. He said he'd wait for me in L.A."

I launched myself at Samantha and wrapped my arms around her. "You came back!"

She pushed me away. "Oh, please, can't you see it's killing me!"

She dropped her suitcase and it fell on my big toe. I was howling with pain and happiness as Samantha ran to our room.

I wanted to go to school. I wanted to see Wesley and practice our play and contemplate our first kiss, but I was too afraid Samantha might change her mind again about leaving, so I stayed home.

I made French toast for breakfast and tried to comfort my sister. She cried a lot, but by lunchtime she'd decided that a separation would be a good test of her and Brian's love. She was practically looking forward to the romantic agony she'd have to endure until June.

In the afternoon we put on our jackets and walked together to the convenience store for a bag of Doritos and some root beer. We got back to the trailer just in time to watch *General Hospital*. The show was halfway over when the phone rang. Samantha was sure it was Brian, but it was Wesley. I dragged the phone into the kitchen with me.

"Mrs. Gober had a minor breakdown because you weren't in class today," Wesley told me.

I sat down on a kitchen chair. "Sorry I wasn't there. Family emergency."

"That's what I thought. I told Mrs. Gober not to worry. I guaranteed her that you know your lines. She invited the principal and the office staff to watch, you know."

"No way."

"She did. And I asked her about changing the ending."

"Well?"

"She asked me if we were trying to improve the play or if we just wanted to kiss each other."

I stopped breathing for so long that I heard my heartbeat in my eardrums. "And? What did you say?"

"I said . . ." Wesley cleared his throat. "I said both."

I jumped up, then fell back down onto the chair. "You did?"

"It's true, right?"

I closed my eyes. "Yes."

The silence between us was full of smiles.

"So, did she say it was okay with her?" I asked.

"She said to go for it. You'd better not be absent tomorrow."

"I won't."

"You promise?"

"Wes. I'll be there."

"Okay. See you in biology, then."

We hung up. When I went back into the living room, Samantha looked up from the TV. "Was that Doug?"

"Nope." I waltzed around the living room with an

invisible partner. "It was my new soon-to-be boyfriend, Wesley Wilton."

Samantha laughed. "The Prez?"

"The one and only!" I yelled as I twirled away down the hall.

chapter
twenty-one

On Tuesday Mrs. Gober's freshman English class performed *The Answer of the Ant,* written by Wesley Wilton and Teresa Dinsmore, starring Wesley Wilton and Teresa Dinsmore. Besides the nonperforming members of the class, the audience included Principal Holling, two guidance counselors, four secretaries, a janitor and Mrs. Irene Wilton.

As I said Marcy's lines, my voice quavered with emotion. I had written the words from my heart and I said them from my heart. I was so moving that one of the secretaries asked Mrs. Wilton for a Kleenex to dab her eyes. I could hardly keep from crying myself.

Then came the end. Wesley was stretched out on Mrs. Gober's desk, which was covered with a sheet to make it look like a bed. His face was wrapped in gauze so that only his eyes and mouth were showing. I became hypnotized by the shiny texture of Wesley's lips as he told me that he would be scarred for life and that he knew I'd never be able to love him.

"Oh, my sweet fool," I said to Wesley/Steve. "My heart decides who I love."

The room fell silent as my face floated down to Wesley's. His eyes were wide open and his tongue darted out to wet his lips just before my mouth reached his. My hand rested on his bandaged jaw and I could feel the pulse in his neck leaping against my little finger as my lips moved over his. My first kiss, in front of thirty people.

Half the class started in with a loud "Ooooo!" I felt Wesley smiling against my lips before I raised my head.

When the play was over, everyone stood and applauded and whistled. Mrs. Wilton came over and hugged us both. Then Mrs. Gober hugged us and Principal Holling shook our hands. No Broadway opening could have been better.

That afternoon, Wesley and I spent an hour on the phone, reliving our glory. We decided that if our play was ever produced again, we would cut out the part about the dead mouse, and add more kisses at the end.

"Better make it four," Wesley said. "We have to make sure we accurately portray the characters' feelings for each other."

"Do you think four is enough?" I asked.

"Probably not," he said, and we fell into one of our smile-filled silences. Then through the kitchen window, I saw Mom's car pull up into the driveway.

"Gotta go," I said.

"Call me back," he said.

"I will."

"Hey, wait," he said.

"What?"

"The spring dance is next Friday."

"I know."

"We should go."

My heart beat faster. "You mean together?"

"Unless you prefer to wave to each other across the room."

"Well, I might."

I heard the front door open. "I gotta go."

"Call me back," he said.

"I will."

By the time I got to the living room, Mom was standing inside the open front door, facing Samantha, who sat on the couch trying to watch *General Hospital*.

"Your grandmother told me you didn't go to L.A. after all," Mom said to her.

Samantha didn't look away from the screen as she said, "Apparently."

Mom forced a cheerful smile. "Well, I'm glad you decided to stay."

Samantha didn't even blink.

Then Andrew came through the door behind Mom and pushed by her. She grabbed for his arm and missed. "Honey, I told you to stay in the car—"

But Andrew was already headed toward me, arms up. I automatically bent down to hug him.

"No!" Mom cried, lunging for him. "Don't touch him. He has head lice."

I jumped back just as Mom grabbed him by the shoulders and pulled him toward the door. He stood grinning between Mom's arms, clearly not too bothered by his condition.

"The school called me this morning," Mom said. "They said they notified Bill about it yesterday and he didn't do a thing about it. I have to take Andrew over to the salon so I can shave his head."

"Freakin' figures," Samantha muttered. But she still didn't look away from the TV.

"Look, Samantha," said Mom, "I know you're angry with me right now. And maybe you have the right to be. It's just that ever since the fire, I..." Her voice trailed off as Samantha picked up the remote and turned the TV up.

Mom looked at me, then looked back at Samantha. "All right," she said more loudly. "I can see you're not interested in what I've been through. And that's fine. I only stopped by because I—Andrew, no!"

Andrew had slipped away from her and was about to sit on Gramma's rocking chair when Mom's yell stopped him.

"Well, where can I sit, then?"

"Here, come sit right here on the floor next to me."

As soon as she got Andrew settled, Mom turned back

to Samantha. "Would you mind turning that down, please?"

When Samantha didn't move, I picked up the remote and turned the TV down myself. I never understood why Samantha had to be rude to make a point.

Mom flashed me a look of thanks. "As I was saying," she began again, "I only stopped by because I wanted to tell you that you do matter to me. And if you don't see that, well then, I'm sorry."

Samantha merely continued gazing at the TV.

Mom took a sharp breath in and let it rush out. Then she squared her shoulders. "You don't want to accept my apology? All right, fine. Don't. I'm tired of defending myself."

With a nod to me, she picked up my brother's hand. "Come on, Andrew, let's go get those bugs out of your hair."

A moment later, we heard her car shoot out of the driveway, spraying gravel.

Samantha slowly shook her head. "She calls that an apology."

"Well," I said. "From her, that's probably as good as you're going to get."

Samantha groaned and stuck her hands to her forehead, making a shelf over her eyes like the brim of a baseball cap. "How about if I *pay* you? I'll pay you a hundred dollars if you'll just *stop* trying to protect Mom."

I sighed. "I'm not trying to protect her."

"Then what would you call it?" She folded her knees up to her chest. "Kissing her butt, maybe?"

I stamped my foot. "I'm not trying to protect Mom! I'm trying to—"

I stopped. I had almost said, "I'm trying to protect me." But why would I say that? Protect myself from what?

I stared at Samantha, balled up on the couch, jaw clenched, radiating anger like heat.

"Just look at you," I said. "What good does it do you to get so mad? It's not like it's going to make her change or anything. It just makes her leave."

"Good," said Samantha. "I'm sick of her."

I shook my head. "I guess you'll never change, either." I turned and went into the kitchen to call Wesley back.

Twenty minutes later, I went back into the living room and found Samantha sitting exactly as I'd left her, knees to her chest, staring vacantly at the TV. I sat in Gramma's rocker to see what was happening on *Oprah*. When a commercial came, Samantha abruptly stood, walked to the phone and dialed. I watched as she tapped her foot, waiting for someone to pick up.

"Gramma," she said finally. "Is Mom still there?" She waited.

"Mom?" she said. "It's me. Okay. Apology accepted."

She didn't wait to hear what Mom would say back.

She hung up the phone, then crossed her arms to look at me. "I'm sure I'll live to regret that."

She went into the bedroom and shut the door.

I was sitting at the kitchen table doing homework when Gramma got home. She stuck her head into the kitchen to say, "Groceries."

I got up to help her carry the bags in from the car. As I unloaded a bag onto the counter, I asked how Andrew was doing.

"Oh, he's a sight, all right," said Gramma as she folded up a paper bag into a rectangle. "More bald than the day he was born."

She handed me the bag, which I stuck in the drawer by my knee.

"After we gave him the treatment, we had to strip him down and keep him in the laundry room, naked as a jaybird." Gramma chuckled. "Your mother finally wrapped him in some towels so he could come out and wait with her for Nolan to drive up."

"Nolan?" I asked. "But why—"

"Well, I couldn't let her go to Bill's for Andrew's things all by herself, now, could I?"

Gramma's face didn't change, but as she folded up another bag, she made extra-neat creases, then held it up to admire it, so I knew she was pleased that Mom was finally getting Andrew back from Bill.

Samantha wandered in, hair messy, as if she'd just

gotten up from a nap. "What's for dinner?" she asked over a yawn.

"Hmmm," Gramma said, peering into a bag. "What strikes your fancy? Pork chops or tuna casserole?"

Before Samantha could answer, a car turned into the driveway and slammed to a skidding halt on the gravel. We looked through the window to see Mom jump out the driver's side of Nolan's car, then run around to the passenger side, where Nolan sat with something blood-soaked pressed to his face.

Gramma gasped, "Good Lord!" and hurried to open the back door. Nolan came in first, head tilted far back, a handkerchief pressed to his nose. Then came Mom, face drawn with worry, followed by a shocking bald Andrew, clinging to Mom's shirt as he bawled.

"What on earth!" Gramma said as she turned to the sink to run water onto a dish towel.

"Nolan hit my daddy!" Andrew wailed.

Samantha smirked as she shut the back door. "Looks like Nolan was the one who got hit."

"It was a lucky punch," Nolan said to the ceiling, his voice muffled by the handkerchief. "He was already on his way down."

"You hurt him!" Andrew cried.

"Damn right I did," said Nolan, which only made Andrew cry harder.

As Mom moved to pull out a kitchen chair and help Nolan grope his way into it, Andrew staggered back and forth behind her, dragged by the fistful of her shirt still in his hand.

"Andrew, honey, you have to let go." Mom reached around to tug at the piece of shirt in his hands, then crouched down to gather him in a hug. She patted his back and whispered, "I know, I know," while he cried.

When he began to calm down, she said, "Your daddy's not hurt bad, sweetie pie, I promise. You know how tough your daddy is. He'll be just fine."

Andrew straightened and his entire head, from his neck to his bare scalp, glowed crimson. He glared at Nolan. "If he hits Daddy again, I'll punch him!"

"Attaboy." Nolan took the handkerchief from his nose and showed a face blood-smeared and swollen from a blackening eye. "A man's gotta protect his family, right?"

Gramma held out the wet dish towel to Mom, but Andrew still clung tightly to her neck.

"Samantha? Teri?" Mom said. "A little help?"

I nodded and crossed over to gently pull at my brother's arms. "Come on, Andrew. Let's go into the living room."

He resisted at first, then finally transferred his arms from Mom's neck to mine. I lifted him up and nudged him to wrap his legs around my waist, then carried him from the kitchen.

I sat in Gramma's chair, Andrew on my lap, his head on my shoulder, and we rocked together, listening as

Mom fussed over Nolan's wounds, and Samantha got Nolan to tell her what it was like to smash Bill's face in, and Nolan convinced Gramma not to call the police.

"It's soft, huh?" Andrew said, and reached up to touch his smooth head. I'd unconsciously been running a finger back and forth over his scalp, and now I rubbed my entire hand over it in a slow circle.

"Yeah," I said. "It's kind of neat."

He pushed himself up to look at me with a tear-streaked face. "Daddy started it. He ran up and he pushed Nolan without saying hi or anything. Why did he do that?"

I gave him a helpless shrug. "I don't know why daddies do what they do. I don't know why mommies do what they do, either. Parents—they're just weird, I guess."

"Yeah," he said. He laid his head back on my shoulder. "Make it go again."

I pushed off the floor with my foot to make the chair rock.

chapter twenty-two

On the one-month anniversary of the fire, Samantha and I decided to walk by our old house on the way home from school. As soon as we neared the beauty shop, our steps began to slow. We exchanged "are you sure you want to do this?" looks. But it was too late to change our minds; we were already there, standing in the exact same spot we'd stood the night of the fire to watch it burn.

Somehow I was surprised to see the house blackened and half eaten away. In my mind I always saw it as it had once been, painted white with green trim, lights shining in the windows, Andrew's toys strewn in the yard.

"We lived there our whole lives," Samantha said.

I let out a slow, shaky breath. "Gramma said they're going to tear it down next week."

"Oh. That's good. I guess."

"Yeah," I said. "I guess."

Gramma had pretty much said the same thing the night before. "We all need to move on," she'd said, and

I'd thought, Yeah, like we have a choice. The fire had sent us all falling into the future, ready or not.

So far, we still hadn't settled. Samantha was still living in Gramma's trailer, but only until she got her diploma in hand and could jump on a bus for Los Angeles and Brian. Andrew was also living at Gramma's trailer, but only until he finished the school year. Then he was supposed to go live with Mom and Nolan in Redding.

As for Mom, she was supposedly living at Nolan's, but she still spent a few nights a week at the trailer. "I want my children to know how important they are to me," she'd say to Gramma, all the while looking straight at Samantha.

I was the only one who planned to stay where I was, but that didn't mean I was settled. I still felt surprised to wake up each morning in a different bed, and put on different clothes, and live the life of a different person. I still felt startled when I looked in the mirror and saw someone I might like to be. And I still sometimes wondered if the people at school who waved at me and acted like my friends were playing tricks on me.

Wesley caught me at it the night of the spring dance. We were standing near the back wall of the half-dark gym, pouring punch into plastic cups for Wesley's mom, when Doug came up to grab two cups.

"Hey, Teri," he said. "How you been? Wanna dance with me later?"

After I stammered a "No, thank you," Wesley turned

an appraising look on me. "You could have said yes. I'm not the jealous type."

I shook my head. "It's not like he really *wanted* to dance with me. Doug—he just likes to be polite."

Wesley kept scrutinizing me like I was a specimen under his microscope.

"What?" I finally snapped.

"I'm just wondering about when Janice asked us to sit at her table earlier. Was she just being polite?"

I shrugged as I picked up another cup. "How should I know?"

"And when I asked you to come to the dance with me? Was I just being polite, too?"

"No," I said, annoyed. "You were my friend before the fire. They—weren't."

"So, in your opinion, people are nice to you only because your house caught fire."

He made it sound ridiculous. My voice sounded weak as I said, "Well. It's possible."

Wesley frowned at me the same way Mr. Reginald did when I gave the wrong answer in class. "It's also possible that they finally figured out the secret you were hiding."

"What are you talking about? What secret?"

He took the half-filled cup of punch from my fingers and set it down. Then he picked up my hands and said, "That you're the most interesting girl in school."

I caught my breath. He was always surprising me

like that, saying wonderful things out of nowhere. Sometimes it made me laugh. That time it made tears jump into my eyes.

Wesley frowned at me. "There you go, acting like a girl again." Then he acted like a boy by kissing me, right beside the punch bowl.

Now I smiled there in front of my burned house, remembering what Wesley had said. Was I—interesting? Maybe. But so what if I hadn't figured it all out yet? Maybe discovering who you are is a process of elimination. First, you have to find out who you're not. So far I'd found out I wasn't Doug's girlfriend. I wasn't a Rowdy or a Holy Roller, either. But that didn't mean I was a Nobody. There were lots of things left over.

Samantha's arm brushed mine as she swung her backpack from her shoulder. She squatted to open it, then pulled out an aerosol can.

"You carry spray paint around," I said without much surprise.

"Duh."

With a quick glance at the beauty shop to make sure Gramma wasn't watching through a window, Samantha approached the house, shaking the can as she went. She stopped for moment, picking her spot, then walked up to the wide blank space of wall between the kitchen and living room windows. She began spraying big red block letters, stopping every few minutes to shake the can. SAMANTHA WAS HERE, she wrote.

She walked back to where I stood, then turned to admire her work. She held the can out to me. I shook my head and held up the Magic Marker I'd dug out of my own backpack, then started toward the house.

Just below Samantha's message, I wrote in much smaller and much neater letters: TERI WAS HERE, TOO. I put the cap back on the marker, then took it off again to add: AND SO WAS ANDREW. Samantha came behind me to see what I'd written. She took the marker from my hand and scribbled one last line: AND JEANETTE WAS HERE SOMETIMES.

She slid me a look as if she expected me to object to the dig at Mom, but I just shook my head and laughed. We backed up a bit and stood together beneath the giant oak in the front yard. A breeze made the new leaves sway over our heads. We could hear its high *whoosh* through the pines that towered all around. Samantha leaned to the side to let her shoulder bump mine. I leaned to bump her back.

We were just picking up our backpacks when Nolan's silver BMW pulled up behind us. Nolan gave us a two-fingered wave from behind the steering wheel. Then he opened the door and got out.

He walked over in his stiff-collared pin-striped shirt and loafers with no socks. He put his hands on his hips to regard the house. "Nice work."

Samantha slung her backpack onto her shoulder. "Thanks. We like it."

"It looks like you've had some practice with graffiti," he said.

"It looks like your shiner is finally going away."

Nolan gingerly touched the yellow smudge beneath his eye left from his fight with Bill.

"Hey," he said. "He's the one that went down."

She smiled blandly. "So you say."

Nolan turned his head to her. "Seriously. Bill Rickman is a dirtbag."

Samantha raised a brow. "Tell us something we don't know."

"All right." He nodded. "You might not know this. I'm *not* a dirtbag."

Samantha gave a short bark of laughter. "Is that why you stopped? To give us this news flash?"

"No. I stopped because I need to talk to Dorinda." He pointed his thumb over his shoulder toward the beauty shop. "Your mother and I are planning a little get-together at our house tomorrow night and would like you all to come."

"How thrilling," said Samantha.

Nolan tilted his head to squint at her. "You don't like me much, do you, Samantha?"

She tilted her head in the same manner, mocking him. "Mom's boyfriends usually aren't so perceptive. But you're deep, Nolan, very deep."

His strained smile told me he was working hard to

hold on to his sense of humor. "At least Teri likes me. Right, Teri?"

I surprised myself by nodding. "Sure. You're all right, I guess."

He smiled big and gave me a friendly whack on the back. "See? I'm one of the good guys, right? And I'd bet big money that by Christmastime, me and ol' Samantha here will be best buds."

"That's *if* you're still around by then," Samantha said.

Nolan's smile dropped away. "Oh, I'll be around, all right. You'll find that out real quick."

He turned and headed toward the beauty shop.

Samantha looked at me and lifted her open palms. "What the hell did *that* mean?"

Nolan marched back toward us. "I'll tell you what it means," he began, finger pointed at Samantha. "It means that tomorrow night we're not just sitting down to dinner. Tomorrow night, me and your mom are getting married."

My backpack slipped from my hands and fell to the ground as Samantha shouted, "What!"

Nolan's pointed finger slowly drifted down as a guilty look stole across his face. "Uh, don't tell your mother I told you. It's supposed to be a surprise."

"You mean a secret," Samantha said.

"Well, yeah, something like that," Nolan said.

"Why?" I asked in a voice that shook. I hoped I

wasn't about to cry. "Why didn't Mom want us to know?"

Nolan sighed. "It's not you. It's our mothers. You know what they're like. It's—well, you see, it's like this." He put his hands out in front of him as if he was holding an invisible football. "The element of surprise is absolutely crucial in getting past the defense."

"What, you don't think your mom wants to be our granny Redmond?" Samantha laughed, then shook her head at me. "Can you believe *this* is our next stepfather?"

She stepped up to Nolan and poked him in the chest. "Just so you know, Mom's husbands don't last much longer than her boyfriends. You might see one Christmas, but I bet you big money that you won't see two." Then she spun and stalked off down the hill.

Nolan sputtered between a laugh and a curse as if he didn't know whether to admire her or smack her. "Is she always like that?"

I nodded. "Pretty much."

"Man," he said.

"Yeah," I agreed.

He turned back to me. "She's wrong about me, you know. I'm not like those other jerks your mother married. I'm going to take care of her. I'm going to make her happy."

Nolan's earnest look almost made me smile. It looked as if Mom had found her Prince Charming after all. And if Nolan was looking for Snow White, he couldn't do better than Mom. He'd probably have to search for years to find another woman who wanted rescuing like she did.

The thought brought an unexpected chill that raised goose bumps on my arms. Either this would be Mom's most successful marriage or it would be her most painful divorce.

I picked up my backpack from the ground. "When you invite Gramma, you should probably tell her about the wedding part. If you don't, Samantha will."

He nodded. "Thanks."

"And hey. Good luck tomorrow."

Nolan gave me his two-fingered wave, then jogged toward the beauty shop as if heading into the Big Game.

That was my next stepfather. Well, I thought, I'd definitely had worse.

As I turned to catch up with Samantha, I looked one last time at what was left of our house. For a moment I could see the flames again, leaping against the night sky, and feel the ashes drifting against my face. And I remembered how terrified I'd been when the fire had started, how I'd crawled coughing through the smoke-filled hall, and how we'd raced through the living room on a rush of adrenaline. I also remembered the relief of tumbling out the front door into the sweet, cold air.

I dragged my eyes away from the house and started down the hill toward my sister. And for the first time it occurred to me that no one had come to rescue us from the fire. Samantha and I, we had rescued ourselves.

about
the author

Teena Booth is a journalist who has edited trade magazines, taught writing in juvenile hall and been a community youth coordinator and a founding board member of a California Big Brothers/Big Sisters organization. She has also served in the air force and in the coast guard. She grew up in Los Angeles and now lives in Phoenix with her husband and three children. *Falling from Fire* is her first novel.

5/28/12